RUBY AT SCHOOL

BY

MRS. GEORGE A. PAULL

RUBY AT SCHOOL

CHAPTER I.

RUBY IN MISCHIEF.

It does seem quite too bad to begin a new Ruby book with Ruby in mischief the very first thing; and yet what can I do but tell you about it? for it is very probable that if she had not been in this particular piece of mischief, this story would never have been written. "Nobody but Ruby would ever have thought of such a thing," Ann exclaimed, when it was discovered, and it really did seem as if Ruby thought of naughty things to do that would never have entered any one else's head.

Ruby had certainly been having one of her "bad streaks," as Nora called her particularly mischievous times, and perhaps this was because Ruby had been left to herself more than she had ever been in all her life before.

Mamma was sick, and she was only able to have Ruby come into her room when the little girl was willing to be very quiet and move about gently, so as not to disturb her; and she knew very little of what Ruby was about in the long hours which she spent in play.

All summer Ruby had been running wild, coming into the house only to eat her meals, or towards evening nestling down beside mamma, to talk to her for a little while about what she had been doing all day. I am afraid it was not very often that Ruby told her of the many things she had been doing of which she knew mamma would not approve at all.

When Ruby went over to Mrs. Warren's house to visit Ruthy, Mrs. Warren tried to have her do as she wished her own little girl to do, but she found it a very much harder matter to govern quick-tempered, impulsive Ruby than it was to guide her own gentle little daughter, and she often sighed as she thought how distressed Ruby's mamma would be if she knew how self-willed and mischievous her little daughter was growing without her mother's care.

Ruby's papa was very busy with his patients, and when he was at home he spent most of his time in the invalid's room, so he did not have any idea how much the little girl needed some one to look after her, and see that she did not get into mischief.

Ann did her best to take care of Ruby, but she had more work to do than usual, so she had very little time to keep watch of the little girl; and besides, Ruby would not mind Ann unless she said she would tell Dr. Harper if Ruby was naughty, and Ann did not like to complain of Ruby if she could help it.

Altogether you can see that Ruby had a pretty good opportunity to be just as naughty as she wanted to be; and every day it did seem as if she thought of more mischievous things to do than she had ever done in all her life put together before.

Ruby was having a very nice time this afternoon all by herself. It would have been nicer to have had Ruthy to help her enjoy it, but Mrs. Warren was not willing to let Ruthy go over to Mrs. Harper's, now that there was no one to see what the two little girls were about. Ruthy could be trusted not to get into any mischief by herself, but sometimes she yielded to Ruby's coaxing when she had devised some piece of mischief, and then no one knew what the two little girls would do next.

Some carpenters had been at work down by the stable, building a new hen-house, and Ruby had made a playhouse for herself with the boards they had left. She had leaned them up against the low branch of an old tree, with Ann's help, for the boards were rather too heavy for her to move alone, and so she had a tent-shaped house of boards in which she thought it was great fun to play.

Ruby's favorite story was the "Swiss Family Robinson," and she thought that no greater happiness could befall any one than to be cast away upon a desert island. As long as there did not seem to be any prospect of a desert island before her, when the largest piece of water she had ever seen in her life was the small shallow pond where the boys got water-lilies in summer, and skated in winter, she thought the next best thing would be to live in this little house, and not go home at all, except to see her mother.

She was very sure that the rest of the family would not approve of this plan at all, so she did not say anything to them about it, but determined to try it and see how she liked it, without running any chances of being forbidden.

One day, when she knew Ann was busy up in her mother's room, and no one would see what she was doing, she ran up to the garret, and brought down a pair of blankets, an old comforter, and the little pillow that belonged to the crib in which she had slept when she was a baby. She carried all these out to her little playhouse in the yard, and has only just tucked away the last corner of the comforter out of sight, when she heard the sound of wheels as her father's buggy drove into the yard.

Ruby ran out to meet him, afraid that he might come and look into her little wooden tent, and see what she had taken from the house. She was very sure that he would not at all approve of her plan of spending the night out there alone. She slipped her hand into his, and walked up to the house with him, and then ran back to her play.

After dinner she chose a time when Nora would not be in the kitchen, and carried some provisions down to her little house; for though she wanted to imitate the Swiss Family Robinson as far as possible, she was not sure that she would be able to find meals for herself as readily as they did; so, though biscuits and cookies were not at all the sort of food shipwrecked people generally eat, she thought that she had better lay in a supply of them, particularly as there were no kindly cocoanut or bread-fruit trees growing at hand.

She filled her apron with the crisp fresh cookies which Ann had just made, and with biscuit from the stone crock, and then spying a little turnover which she was sure Ann had made for her, she added that to her store.

It began to look quite like a castaway's tent, Ruby imagined, as she sat down in her little house and looked around. To be sure, you would hardly expect any one wrecked upon a desert island to have such a comfortable roof of boards over his head, and certainly one would not find a supply of warm, dry bed-clothing at hand, nor fresh cookies; but Ruby was quite satisfied, and she thought it would be great fun to spend the night out there all by herself, and imagine herself in the midst of a forest all alone. She shut her eyes, and as the wind rustled the branches of the tree, she pretended that she heard the waves breaking upon the shore of her desert island, and that chattering monkeys were jumping about over her head in the branches of great palm and tall cocoanut-trees.

If Ruthy could only be cast away with her it would be ever so much nicer, for then she would not have to enjoy it all by herself; but she reflected that it was just as well that Ruthy could not come over and play, for she probably would be afraid to sleep out there, and would cry and want to go into the house just when the play grew the most interesting.

No thought of fear entered venturesome Ruby's mind. It would be an easy matter for her to slip out of the house after she was supposed to be fast asleep in her trundle bed, which was not beside her mother's bed any longer, but in a room by itself. Ruby did not know that the the last thing her father did every night before he went to bed, was to go and take a look at his little girl, and see that she was sleeping comfortably; and very often he went into her room in the evening, soon after she had gone to sleep.

Of course she knew that she was going to do a naughty thing, but I am sorry to say that Ruby did not very often let that interfere with anything she wanted to do now, she had her own way so much.

She was so excited over her plan for the night that she was very quiet all the rest of the afternoon, and Ann said rather suspiciously,—

"You're up to some new mischief, Ruby Harper, I'll venture, or you would never be so quiet all at once. I know you. Now do be a good girl, and don't keep worrying your poor ma so about you."

"Never you mind what I am going to do," answered Ruby, pertly, and just then Ann saw that her cookies were missing.

"Well, where on earth are all my cookies?" she exclaimed. "Now, Ruby Harper, you tell me this very minute what you have been doing with them. I know just as well as anything that you never ate such a lot as that, and I don't see what you could have been doing with them. You go and get them and fetch them back to me right away."

Ruby made a face at her and darted away. She was not going to bring the cookies back nor tell where they were. What would she do when she was shipwrecked if she did not have a store of provisions in her hut, as she called her little house.

She knew it would not do to tell Nora about her plan, and she was so full of it that she felt as if she could not keep it to herself any longer, so she ran over to Ruthy's house.

She found Ruthy playing with her paper dolls on the wide back porch, and for a few minutes she pretended that she had come over to see her paper nieces and nephews, for the children always called themselves aunts to each other's dolls.

"Oh, I have got a plan to tell you about, Ruthy," she said presently. "I don't want any one to hear me telling you about it, so let's go down under the apple-tree, with the dolls."

Ruthy gathered up her children, and in a few moments the two little girls were sitting side by side on the low bench, which Ruthy's father had put there just for their comfort.

"It's the grandest plan," began Ruby.

"Am I in it, too?" asked Ruthy, half wistfully and half fearfully. She always liked to be in Ruby's plans, and felt a little left out when her little friend wanted to do without her, and yet sometimes Ruby's plans were so very extraordinary that she did not enjoy helping to carry them out at all.

"Well, you could be in it, only you see you can't very well," Ruby answered in a rather mixed up fashion.

"Why can't I?" Ruthy asked.

"Well, I'll tell you all about it, and then you will see that you couldn't very well," Ruby answered. "But first of all you must promise me honest true, black and blue, that you will never, never breathe a word of it to any one."

"Not even to mamma?" asked Ruthy, who always felt better when she told her mother all about everything.

"No, not to anyone in all the wide world," Ruthy answered. "I won't tell you a single word unless you promise, and you will be awfully sorry if I don't tell you, for this is the most splendid plan I ever made up in all my life. It is just like a book."

Ruthy's curiosity overcame her scruples about knowing something which she could not tell her mother.

"All right, I won't tell a single person," she said, earnestly. "Tell me what it is."

"Promise across your heart," Ruby insisted, for just then the little girls had a fashion of thinking that promising across their hearts made a promise more binding than any other form of words.

"I promise, honest true, black and blue, 'crost my heart," Ruthy said very earnestly, and then the two heads were put close together while Ruby whispered her wonderful secret.

No one could have heard them, not even the birds in their nests up in the tree, if she had spoken aloud, but a secret always seemed so delightfully mysterious when it was whispered, that she rarely told one aloud.

"I am going to be cast away on a desert island," she said, and Ruthy's blue eyes opened to their widest extent.

"Why, how can you, when there is n't any desert island anywhere near here for miles and miles?" she exclaimed.

"Oh, you are so stupid," Ruby exclaimed impatiently. "Of course I mean to pretend I am cast away. I am going to pretend that down by the barn is a desert island, and that little house I have built with boards is my hut, and I am going to sleep out there all by myself to-night, and I have some provisions and everything all ready."

"But will you dare stay out there all alone when it gets dark?" asked Ruthy in awed tones, feeling quite satisfied that she was left out of this plan, for she knew she should never dare to do such a thing, no matter how much Ruby might want her to join her.

CHAPTER II.

CARRYING OUT HER PLAN.

"Of course I would dare," answered Ruby, positively. "I am not such a coward as you are, Ruthy. You see, even if your mamma would let you come over and stay at my house, so you could be in the plan, it would n't be of any use, for it would be just like you to get afraid as soon as it was dark, and then you would cry and want to go back into the house."

"I am afraid I would," Ruthy answered meekly, not resenting the accusation of cowardice. "I should think you would be afraid too, Ruby; and then what will your papa and mamma think when they find out in the night that you are gone."

"They won't find out," answered Ruby, easily disposing of that objection. "You see I shall wait till after they think I have gone to sleep to go out to my hut. I will get most undressed to-night at bed-time and then put my nightie on over the rest of my clothes, and when papa comes in to kiss me good-night he will never think of my getting up again. Then I will creep downstairs as softly as a mouse, and out into the yard. It will be such fun to roll up in the blankets, and pretend that they are the skins of wild animals, and I shall lie awake for ever so long listening to hear if any bears come around, or lions. Oh, it will be such fun," and Ruby's eyes sparkled. Ruthy looked troubled.

"I don't think it will be a bit nice," she said presently. "I don't believe your mamma would like it one single bit; and suppose somebody should carry you off when you are out there all by yourself."

"You just can't make me afraid, I guess, Ruthy Warren," sniffed Ruby, scornfully. "You are such a 'fraid-cat that you never want to do anything in all your life but play paper dolls. I might have known you would n't see what fun it is to play Swiss Family Robinson. Now don't you dare tell any one a single word about it. Remember you promised across your heart."

"I sha'n't tell," Ruthy answered, "but I do wish you would n't do it, Ruby. Why, I shall be as scared as anything if I wake up in the night and think that you are out there in your house all alone in the pitch dark. I should be so frightened if I was you that I would just scream and scream till some one heard me and came and got me."

"I would n't have such a baby as you to stay with me," Ruby said. "I am going to do it just as sure as anything, Ruthy Warren, and if you breathe a word of it to any one so I don't get let to do it, I will never, never speak to you again as long as I live and breathe."

"Of course I sha'n't tell when I promised," Ruthy replied, a little hurt at Ruby's doubting her word. "Maybe you won't do it after all, though. Perhaps when it gets dark you will be frightened."

"I never get frightened," Ruby said, tossing her head. "Now I must go home, Ruthy. Come and walk part way with me, won't you?"

"I'll ask mamma," Ruthy answered, and gathering up her paper dolls she ran into the house, coming back in a few minutes with two red-cheeked apples for the little girls to eat on their way, and permission to go as far as the corner with Ruby.

Ruby could talk and think of nothing but her great plan for the night, and Ruthy pleaded with her in vain to give it up. The little girl was so troubled about it that she wished Ruby had not told her about it. She did not see how she would ever be able to go to bed that night, and go to sleep, thinking of her little friend out alone in her little house down by the barn. In the bottom of her heart she wished that Ruby would be caught by Ann on her way out of the house, and prevented from carrying out her plan, but she did not dare whisper this wish to Ruby, as she knew how angry it would make her to think of her plans being thwarted.

By the time Ruby reached home another plan occurred to her busy brain. Nora was not far from right when she said that Ruby could think up more mischief than any three children could carry out. Suppose it should be cold in the night. Ruby could not quite remember what time in the year it was when the Swiss Family Robinson were shipwrecked, but she knew they had to make a fire. She would get some shavings and some little sticks, and get a fire all ready to light in her hut, and then if it should be cold, and she should want to light a fire, it would be all ready.

This new idea added a great charm to the thought of staying out there all night. She was quite sure that she would need a fire, and she bustled around very busily when she got home, gathering up shavings from the place where the carpenters had been at work, and getting little sticks to lay upon them so that the fire would burn up readily. Then she went back to the house, and going up into the spare room, took down the match-box from the tall chest of drawers, and carried it out to the hut where it would be all ready for the night. When this was done she felt as if she could hardly wait for the sun to go down and bedtime to come. She was so excited over her grand plan that her eyes shone like stars, and her cheeks were so flushed that when her father came in, he put his hand on her cheeks to see whether she had any fever. If he had only known what a naughty plan was in Ruby's mind, he would have been more sorry than to have had his little girl sick.

Of course I need not tell you that Ruby knew just how wrong it was to plan something which she knew very well her father and mother would not permit for a moment if they knew of it. But in all the years that you have known her she had not grown any less self-willed, I am sorry to say, and so she thought of nothing but of getting her own way, whether it was naughty or not.

The longest day will have an end at last, and though it seemed to Ruby as if a day had never passed so slowly, yet finally the sun went down. Ruby had had her supper, had kissed mamma good-night, and bed-time had come. She took off her shoes, and her dress, and then slipping her little white night-dress on over her other clothes, she scrambled into bed, and waited for her papa to come and kiss her good-night, her heart beating so loudly with excitement that she was afraid he would hear it, and wonder what was the matter with her. I think if it had been her mother who had come in she would have wondered why only Ruby's dress and shoes were to be seen, and why the little girl had such a flushed, guilty look, and held the bed-clothes tucked up so tightly under her chin; but Ruby's papa did not notice any of these things, so Ruby was not hindered from carrying out her naughty plan.

She waited for what seemed to her a very long time, and then she heard the wheels of her father's buggy going out of the yard, and knew he had gone somewhere to see a patient. She was glad, for that made one person less who would be likely to hear her when she went out. Her mamma she was sure would not hear her, for her door was closed, and if she could only get past the kitchen door without Ann discovering her, she would be safe. When she could not hear any one stirring, she got up and crept softly over to the door. The house was very still, so even the rustle of her night-dress seemed to make a noise as she stepped along the hall. Down the stairs she crept like a little thief, and at last she reached the door. Ann had been sitting with her back to the kitchen door reading when Ruby went past, so she had not noticed the little figure gliding along.

Ruby stepped through the open door out upon the back porch. It was dark, and the noise of the tree toads and frogs seemed to make it more lonely than she had thought it would be. For a moment she was almost willing to give up her plan and go back to bed like a good little girl, but then she thought of Ruthy, and how she would hate to confess to her the next day that she had given up her plan after all; so she went on. Ruby was not inclined to be timid about anything, so, although it did not seem as delightful as she had imagined it would, yet she was not afraid as she ran down the yard to her little house. She was glad, however, that it was not upon a desert island. It was very nice to know that she was not surrounded by great rolling waves on every side, and that if she wished to go back to her home and her mother she could do so in a very few minutes.

She crept into her hut, and finding the bedclothes rolled herself up in them. Oh, why was n't it as nice as she had thought it would be? Ruby was provoked with herself for wishing that she was back in the house curled up in her own little bed, instead of being out here in the night alone. She would not give up and go back, though, she said over and over again to herself. No; she had said that she would stay out all night, and she meant to keep her word, whether she liked it or not.

If Ruby had only been half as determined to keep her good resolutions as she was to keep her bad ones, she would never have found herself in such scrapes.

She rolled herself up in a little ball and drew the blanket closely about her,—not because she was cold, but because it seemed less lonesome. While she was listening to all the music of a summer's night, she fell asleep, and dreamed a very remarkable dream about sleeping in a nest swung from a cocoanut-tree, with a monkey for a bed-fellow.

In the mean time very unexpected events were taking place at the house. A little while after Ruby's father had gone out to see his patient a carriage drove up from the station with a visitor.

It was Ruby's Aunt Emma, who had come to make a visit of a few days, and who had written to say that she was coming, but had only discovered at the last moment that her letter had not been mailed in time for her brother to receive it before her arrival.

After she had had a little talk with Ruby's mother, she was very impatient to see her little niece.

"I wish I could have reached here in time to see her before she went to sleep," she said.

"I am afraid if she woke up now and found you were here she would not go to sleep again all night," said Ruby's mother.

"I won't wake her, but I will just go and peep at her while she is asleep," said Aunt Emma; and lighting a candle, she followed Ann into the room where Ruby was supposed to be fast asleep in her trundle-bed.

Of course there was no Ruby there. The little girl was curled up in her blankets out in the yard, under her little tent of boards; and there was only a little crumpled place in the pillow to show where her head had nestled.

"Why, where can she be, I wonder?" said Ann in surprise.

"Hush! don't let her mother hear, or she will be worried," said Aunt Emma, who knew how easily the invalid would be alarmed. "Perhaps she has gone downstairs to get a drink of water or something."

"No, I am sure she has n't been downstairs, for I have been sitting right there in the kitchen all the evening," said Ann, positively. "Oh, Miss Emma, she has got to be the witchiest girl ever you did see. She's always up to some piece of mischief or another, and it's more than any one but her mother can do to keep her in order. I try my best, but it ain't any use at all. She does just as she likes for all of me, unless I tell her father; and then it worries him so that I don't like to, when he has so much else on his mind."

"I should like to know where she is now," said Miss Emma, looking very much puzzled. "There comes her father," she went on, as she heard the sound of wheels coming into the yard. "Perhaps he will know." She went downstairs softly, and met the doctor who, was very much surprised at this unexpected visitor. After he had told her how glad he was to see her, she told him that Ruby was not upstairs in her bed, and that Ann did not know where she was, and asked him if he knew what had become of the little girl.

He looked very anxious.

"Why, no, I have not the least idea," he said gravely. "I kissed her good-night just before I went out to make a call, and she was all right in her bed then. I do not see what could have become of her. I hope we can keep it from her mother, or she will be sadly frightened if she hears Ruby is not to be found at this hour of the night."

Of course no one could imagine where Ruby had gone, and although they hunted all over the house, there was not a trace of the little girl to be seen.

"Perhaps she has been walking in her sleep," suggested Aunt Emma. "She may have wandered downstairs and out into the yard while she was asleep, and been too frightened when she woke up to know how to find her way back into the house. I have heard of children doing such things."

"But she could n't have gone past the door without my seeing her," said Ann, very positively. "I have been sitting right there in the kitchen all the evening, and I am sure I would have heard her, if she had gone past. I never knew Ruby to walk in her sleep; but then I would n't say she might n't have done it this time, only I know she did n't walk past the kitchen door and go out that way."

"Could she have gone out the front door?" asked Aunt Emma.

The doctor shook his head.

"No; that would be too heavy for her to open alone, after it was locked up for the night. I fastened it myself before I went out, and it is fastened now; so she could not have gone out that way. There is her mother calling. I hope she will not ask for Ruby. She must not have this anxiety if we can spare her."

CHAPTER III.

LOOKING FOR RUBY.

People who are sick are very quick to hear when anything is wrong, and as soon as the doctor opened the door of the sick-room, Ruby's mamma asked anxiously,—

"Is anything wrong with Ruby? Where is she?"

Just then the only possible explanation of her absence occurred to the doctor, and he answered,

"She is not in her bed, my dear, and I am afraid she has run away and gone over to Ruthy's to spend the night. You know she asked permission to stay all night the last time she went over there for supper, and I suppose she has made up her mind to go without permission. It is too bad in her to act this way and worry you. I will drive over after her right away, and bring her back in a few minutes."

"I don't believe she would go all the way up to Ruthy's after dark," said her mother, in anxious tones. "I am afraid something has happened to her, though I cannot imagine what it could be."

"Don't think about it till I bring her back safe and sound," said the doctor as he hurried away.

But it was a great deal easier to give this advice than to follow it. Ruby's mamma could not help worrying about her little girl, and while naughty little Ruby was curled up in her blankets, sleeping as sweetly as a little bird in its nest, her mamma was listening to the wheels of the doctor's buggy, rolling out of the yard, with a beating heart, and wondering what had happened to the little girl who had gone to bed not two hours ago.

It did not take very long to drive over to Ruthy's house, and the doctor did not wait to hitch staid old Dobbin, but jumped out and ran up the steps to the house, anxious to know whether Ruby was really there. Although he was quite sure that she must be, yet he was impatient to satisfy himself.

"Is Ruby here?" were his first words, when Mr. Warren opened the door.

"Why, no," Mr. Warren answered. "I don't think she has been here to-day."

"Oh, yes, she was here a little while this afternoon," said Mrs. Warren coming to the door. "Why, what is the matter, doctor? Is n't Ruby at home?"

"No, she went to bed all right, but a little while ago when her aunt came and went to look for her, she was gone," said the doctor, feeling as if he did not know now where to turn to look for the little runaway; for where could she possibly be at that time of night, if she had not come over to visit her little friend? "Where can the child be?"

"Is n't she in the house somewhere?" asked Mrs. Warren.

"No, we have looked through the house," the doctor answered. "I don't know what will become of her mother, if I have to go back without Ruby. No one could have come into the house and stolen her, that is certain, and yet I cannot conceive where she could have gone to at this hour in the evening. This is dreadful."

Neither Mr. Warren nor his wife could suggest any place to look for Ruby. It was certainly a very strange thing that she could have disappeared from her bed after dark, without any one knowing anything about it. The doctor got into his buggy again and started towards home, wondering what he should do when he had to tell Ruby's mother that her little girl could not be found.

If Ruby could have known what a heartache her father had, as he drove slowly homeward, dreading to take such sad news back with him, I am quite sure the little girl would have tried to be good, and not make those who loved her so anxious about her.

In the mean time, Ruby had stirred uneasily in her sleep, and at last when the owl who lived in the tall elm-tree close by, gave a long, mournful hoot, she awakened, and sat up, wondering, as she rubbed her eyes open, where she was.

The cool evening breeze fanned her face, and the stars looked down upon her, and all at once Ruby remembered where she had gone to sleep. In the very depths of her heart she wished that she was back again in her own little bed, with her head on her pillow, and the white spread drawn over her. It seemed so very, very desolate to be down here at the end of the garden all alone, with a long, dark walk before her if she should go back to the house; and she began to think that the Swiss Family Robinson had a better time than Robinson Crusoe, since they were all together, and poor Crusoe must often have been very lonely all by himself, before his man Friday came to live with him.

If Ruthy had only been there, Ruby thought she would have made a very good man Friday, but she was quite sure that nothing would have persuaded Ruthy to stay out of doors at night.

"I am not a little 'fraid-cat like Ruthy," said Ruby to herself, trying to pretend that she was not at all lonely nor frightened. "I would just as lief stay out here every night. I wonder what time it is. I guess it must be nearly morning. I was asleep just hours and hours, I think. I am dreadfully hungry, so it must be ever so long since I had my supper. I had better eat some provisions, maybe."

Ruby was not really very hungry, but she wanted to be as much like the Swiss Family Robinson as possible, so she sat up and sleepily nibbled at some cookies.

"I don't think these are very nice cookies," she said, as she tried to keep up the pretence that she was very hungry. "I wish they were cocoanuts. They would be ever so much nicer."

"I wish this was a big, tall cocoanut-tree," Ruby went on. "And that it was just full of cocoanuts, and that some monkeys had a nest in it, and would throw me down cocoanuts whenever I wanted one. It would hurt if they hit me on the head though. I guess I would have to live under another tree, so as to be sure the cocoanuts would n't drop on me. I wonder if monkeys live in nests. Of course they don't live in bird's-nests, but maybe they take sticks up into trees, and make little nests, and—and—"

Ruby nodded so hard that she woke up again. She had nearly gone to sleep sitting straight up, she was so sleepy.

"I don't want to go to sleep just yet," she said. "I am going to stay awake, so. I might just as well be in bed as keep asleep out here all the time. I guess I will make a fire, and then that will be just like a real castaway."

The sticks and matches were all ready, and Ruby struck a match and lighted the little fire. It was not a very large pile of sticks, and Ruby had not thought that it would make much of a blaze, but the shavings underneath, and the light, dry sticks upon the top, were very ready to take fire and make as large a blaze as they could, so Ruby was quite dismayed at the size of her fire.

She was a little frightened, too. She had made the fire in the front of her little house, and she could not get past it to go out. The fence made a strong back wall to the house, over which she could not climb, and she could not possibly get away from the smoke and heat without going so near the fire that she was sure her night-gown would take fire.

Suppose the boards that she used in making the house should take fire, what would become of her then. I do not wonder that Ruby was frightened when she looked at the little bonfire, crackling and snapping away as cheerily as if a frightened child was not watching it with tears in her eyes.

"Oh, I shall be all burned up," she cried. "And no one will ever know what became of me. My mamma will cry and cry and wonder where Ruby is, but she will never think that I came down here and made a fire, and burned myself all entirely up. Oh, oh, I do wish I had n't. I do wish I had n't. I wonder if I screamed and screamed for papa, whether he would come down and hear me and come down and get me out. Perhaps he could n't. I don't see how anybody could get past that dreadful blaze. He would just have to see me all burning up and he could n't do one thing to save me. Oh, how sorry he would be," and Ruby cried harder than ever at the thought of her father's distress.

The smoke made her eyes smart and sting, and it choked her so that she coughed and strangled, and I need not tell you that she would have given anything in the world to have been back in her own little bed again.

Just then papa drove through the gate, and you can imagine how much surprised he was to see a fire under some boards down at the end of the yard. He jumped out of the buggy and went down there as quickly as he could, to find out what it was.

He looked into the little house, and there beyond the fire, crying so hard that she did not see nor hear him, was the little girl he had been looking for.

"Why, Ruby!" he exclaimed in amazement; and Ruby looked up, as much surprised at finding her father there, as he had been a second before when he saw her.

"Oh, papa, papa, must I be all burned up?" she cried, but papa was already answering that question. He threw down the boards out of which Ruby had made her house, and striding past the fire, lifted her in his arms, and started up to the house with her.

He was so glad that he had found her, and could take her back to her mother safe and unharmed, that he forgot everything else, and of course, Ruby was happy at being in those strong arms, when she had been so sure that she was going to be burned up; and all the way up to the house she resolved, as she had so many times before, that she would surely, surely be good now, for whenever she was naughty, and did things that she knew would not please her father and mother, she always got into trouble, and was not half as happy as she would have been if she had tried to please them. After all, papas and mammas did know what was best for little girls.

CHAPTER IV.

CONSEQUENCES.

Ruby really had very good reason to be sorry for this last piece of naughtiness. By the time her papa carried her into the house they found that her mamma was very ill with the anxiety about Ruby, and her papa just let her kiss the white face once, and then he hurried her away to bed, so that he might do all that he could for the invalid.

Ruby was very much surprised to find every one up in the house. She had been so sure that it was nearly morning that she could not understand how it was that, after all she had been doing, and the long sleep she had had out in her little cabin, it should only be a little after ten o'clock.

It was some time before Ruby went to sleep, and in that quiet time she had a good opportunity to think how very naughty she had been. "I wish I had n't played Swiss Family Robinson," she said to herself. "I wish I had never, never heard anything about that old book. I should never have thought of it by myself, and then, of course, I would never have done such a thing. And now, it is just perfectly dreadful. I know papa thinks I have been too bad to love any more, and mamma is so sick, and Ann looked as cross at me as if she would just like to bite my head off, and I most know she will scold and scold at me to-morrow, and there, Aunt Emma had to come the first time I ever did such a thing, and now, I suppose she thinks I run away every night, and I never, never did before, and it is n't fair, so;" and Ruby cried softly. "Oh, dear, I do wish I had n't, and it don't make the least speck of difference how many times I wish I had n't now, 'cause it is too late. I wish I always knew beforehand how sorry I would be, and then I would n't do things that make me feel so dreadful bad. I wish I knew how mamma is. If she was n't sick, she would come and love me, and make me feel better; she always does when I have been doing things. It is n't my fault if I do bad things. When my mamma's sick, how can I help doing things. I should n't think anybody would 'spect me to mind Ann, cause she's so cross, and anyway she is n't my mamma, so she need n't pretend that she can tell me when I must n't do things. I won't let anybody but my mamma tell me what I must n't do, 'cept maybe my papa. I think it will be too bad for people to scold me for going out to-night, when I never had one bit a nice time. I can tell Ruthy I went, though, anyway, and she will be just as 'sprised, and she will say, 'I don't see how you ever dared, Ruby Harper.' Ruthy would n't dare go out in the dark. She is a real little 'fraid-cat, that is what she is. I 'm glad I am not so 'fraid of everything."

Ruby flounced about upon her pillow. She wanted to find fault with some one else, so as not to have to listen to what her conscience was telling her about herself, but it was not of much use to try to find fault with gentle little

Ruthy. Ruby knew that even if she had not been afraid of going out in the dark, she would never have done anything that she knew would make her mamma and papa feel so badly. Ruthy did things sometimes that she ought not to do, and sometimes forgot her tasks, but it was rarely, if ever, that she deliberately planned a piece of mischief; and if she was concerned in one, it was almost always because Ruby had coaxed her into it.

"If Ann was n't so cross, I don't believe I would do so many things," Ruby went on, still trying to find some one else to blame. "I never did so many things when mamma was well. I am going to ask her to send Ann away, 'cause it is her fault."

But Ruby know better than that. It was because she was so very sure that it had been all her fault that she had done something that she had known perfectly well would displease her mamma and papa if they should know it, and that had worried her papa and made her mamma worse, that she was so anxious to lay the blame upon some one else.

She turned her pillow over and over, and thumped it at last, she grew so impatient because she could not go to sleep.

"I don't think it is very pleasant to stay awake all night, and keep thinking about things," she said. "Oh, dearie me, I do wish I was asleep. I wonder if people think when they are asleep. They can't tell whether they do think or not, I s'pose, 'cause they 're asleep and don't know it. I wish I was asleep, anyway. I wish I had n't gone down into that yard. I guess I do know I ought n't to have done it, and I am just as sorry as I can be. I could n't be any more sorry if papa should call me Rebecca Harper, and scold me like everything, and if mamma should scold me, too. I guess I won't say anything even if Ann scolds me, for I know I ought not to have done such a dreadful thing. Suppose I had been all burned up; and that is just what would have happened if my papa had not come! I wonder how he happened to come down into the yard and see the fire. I never s'posed he would come. I thought I was just going to be all burned up, so I did. Was n't it dreadful to be so close to a fire, and not be able to get away? I would have been all burned up by this time, and my house would have been all burned up, too, and no one would ever have known what became of me. Mamma would always have said, 'I wonder where Ruby could possibly have gone, and why she never, never comes home,' and papa would worry and worry, and Ruthy would have been so lonely, and they would never, never have known."

At the thought of such sad consequences to her mischief, Ruby cried a little, and before her tears had dried, she was fast asleep, so she did not know how ill her mamma was all night, nor how great had been the consequences of her mischief.

In the morning when Ruby waked up, she found Ann by her bedside.

"Here is your breakfast," said Ann, putting down a tray with Ruby's bowl of bread and milk upon it, on a little table. "Your papa says you are to stay here till he comes up and lets you out. Oh, Ruby, how could you be so naughty and worry your poor mamma? You don't know how sick you made her with your cutting up."

Ann did not speak angrily, but she seemed to feel so badly about Mrs. Harper's illness that Ruby felt very subdued and did not try to defend herself as usual.

"I don't want to stay up here. I want to go down and eat my breakfast with Aunt Emma," she said, presently, turning her head away, so Ann might not see the tears which were coming into her eyes.

"Your papa said you must stay up here," Ann repeated, and without saying anything more, she went out, and Ruby heard the bolt slide, and knew that she was a prisoner.

"I don't like to be locked in. I just won't be," she said angrily; and she thought she would jump up and go and pound at the door until some one should come to unfasten it; but then she remembered how sick Ann had said her mamma was, and she knew that a noise would disturb her; and more than that,—it would make her feel so badly to know that Ruby was in a temper.

There was something else that Ruby remembered, too. The last time her papa had told her to stay in her own room till he should come to let her out, he had trusted her and had not fastened the door; and when he went upstairs, he had found that Ruby had gone out, and was down in the yard playing with her kitten, just as if she was not in disgrace; so it was no wonder that he could not trust her this time. Ruby sat down on the side of the bed very meekly when she remembered all this, and I am glad to say, really resolved that as far as she could she would make up for having been so naughty last night, by trying to be as good as possible now, and not give any more trouble to her mother.

Downstairs her father and Aunt Emma were eating their breakfast, and her father was saying sadly,—

"I am sure I don't know what to do with the child. I am so busy with my patients that I can hardly take the time to be with her mother as much as I should be, and Ann does not seem to be able to make her mind. I know she is always getting into mischief, and she certainly does seem to think of more extraordinary things to do than any child I ever knew. She might have been badly burned last night, if I had not seen the blaze, and even if she had escaped herself, the fire might have spread to the boards and fence, and then there is no knowing where it would have stopped. Her mother will never get well while she worries about Ruby, and you see for yourself what harm last night worry did her. I declare I don't know what to do."

"I have a plan," said Aunt Emma, after a little thought. "I will take Ruby back to school with me."

CHAPTER V.

BOARDING-SCHOOL.

"Take Ruby to school with you?" repeated Dr. Harper in surprise.

"Yes, I think that is the only thing to be done," Aunt Emma answered. "Of course you would miss her, but you would know that she was in safe keeping, and that I would take good care of her, and make her as happy as possible; and then without the anxiety of her whereabouts or her doings upon her mind, her mother would have a better chance to get well. You see you never can know what the child will do next, and if she had not made that fire she might not have been found until morning, and you know in what a state her mother would have been by that time. I have a week yet before I must go back to teach, and I will get her ready and take her back with me."

At first it seemed to Dr. Harper as if he could not possibly let his only little daughter go away to boarding-school, even with her aunt, but as he thought more about it, and talked it over with Aunt Emma, he decided that it was the only thing to do with self-willed, mischievous little Ruby, until her mother should be better again, and able to control her.

The next thing to do was to secure her mother's consent, and Dr. Harper said,—

"I am afraid it will take some time to persuade her that she can let Ruby go away from her. She will miss her so much, and will worry lest Ruby should be homesick."

He was very much surprised, when he suggested the plan, to hear her say,—

"That is just what I have been thinking about myself. If I only knew that she was being taken good care of, and could not get into any more mischief, I would be willing to let her go, for I shall never have another easy moment about her while I am too sick to take care of her myself. I do not know what she will do next."

That was just the trouble. Nobody ever knew what Ruby was going to do next, and as she generally got into mischief first, and then did her thinking about it afterwards, one might be pretty sure that she would carry out any plan that came into her head, whatever its consequences might be.

Dr. Harper was seriously displeased with his little daughter, and he determined to give her ample time to think over her naughty conduct; so after he had eaten his breakfast, and done all that he could for the invalid, he went out to visit his patients, leaving her shut up in her room, where she could not get into any more mischief for a few hours at any rate.

Ruby had dressed herself and eaten her breakfast, feeling very lonely and penitent, and then she expected that her papa would come and let her out. She wanted to go in to her mamma's room and tell her how sorry she was that she had worried her so the night before; but the minutes went by, and still her father did not come, and when at last Ruby heard his buggy wheels going past the house, she knew that he meant to leave her by herself until he should come back.

It seemed a long, long time to Ruby, though it was only two hours really, and she had time to think of all that had happened, and all that might have happened before her papa came back.

Ruby heard him drive around to the stable, and she knew just about how long it would take him to walk up to the house. Presently she heard his step upon the porch, and then he came upstairs, and went first into her mother's room, to see how she was, and then after a few minutes he came out, and Ruby heard him coming towards her room. The moment he opened the door she ran and threw herself into his arms.

"I am so sorry; indeed I am sorry, papa," she cried, bursting into tears.

Her father sat down, and took her up on his knee.

"And you have made us all very sorry, Ruby," he answered. "Your mother is very much worse, because she had such a fright last night. Just think what it was when we thought you were safely asleep for the night to find that you had disappeared, without any one knowing where you had gone. I drove over to Ruthy's to look for you; and I do not know what I should have done if I had not seen the fire, and found you in the yard. I should not have had the least idea where to look for you; and I do not think you can realize what serious consequences your naughtiness might have had. And they might have been very dangerous ones to yourself too. If your clothes had taken fire, as they easily might have done, I cannot bear to think what would have happened to my little daughter."

Ruby cried on, with her face hidden in her father's shoulder.

"Oh, I am so sorry. You can do anything you like to me, papa; indeed, you can," she sobbed. "Perhaps you don't b'lieve how sorry I am, but I never was more sorry for anything; never, never."

"I know you are sorry, Ruby," said her father. "You are always sorry after you have done wrong; but that does not seem to keep you from getting into the next piece of mischief that comes into your head. I cannot let you go on in this way any longer. For your mother's sake, if not your own, I must put a stop to it, or she will never have a chance to get well. I am going to send you away to boarding-school with your Aunt Emma."

"Oh, papa, papa, don't do that! please don't!" exclaimed Ruby, clinging to him. "I don't want to go away from you and mamma. I don't! oh, I don't! Please let me stay home, and you can keep me shut up in this one single room all the time, and I won't say one word; truly, I won't; but do let me stay with you and mamma. I will be so good."

"You think you will now, Ruby; but in a few days you would be in as much mischief as ever. It is better for you to be where some one can take care of you. As soon as your mother is better you shall come home again; and after a few days, I have no doubt but that you will be very happy there with Aunt Emma and the new friends you will make."

"I don't believe Ruthy will like to go," said Ruby presently, after a little thought.

"Ruthy is not going, my dear," answered her father.

"Oh, isn't Ruthy going?" asked Ruby, in surprise. "I thought of course Ruthy would go if I did. Oh, papa, I can't go without Ruthy. I truly can't. Won't you make her go with me? Please do; and then I will try not to cry about going."

"I don't believe Ruthy's papa and mamma would want to spare her," answered the doctor. "But you will be with Aunt Emma, you know, dear; and you love her, and she will take very good care of you."

"But I want Ruthy, too," Ruby said, looking very much as if she was going to begin crying again at the thought of being separated, not only from her father and mother, but from her little friend as well.

"Now Ruby, dear, if you are really sorry that you have been so naughty," said her father, "you will show it by doing all you can to be good now. If you fret and cry and worry about going to school, it will make it very hard for your mother, and perhaps make her worse. If you had been good, and tried to do what you knew would please her when she was not able to watch you, it would not have been necessary to send you away; but you have shown that you need some one to look after you, so there does not seem to be any other way but this of giving your mother a chance to get well without unnecessary anxiety; and of making sure that you are not doing every wild thing that comes into your head. I do not think Ruthy can go with you; so you must try to make the best of things, and go with your Aunt Emma without complaining. If you will do this, I shall know that you really love your mamma and want to do all you can to make her better; and then just as soon as she is well, you shall come home again."

Ruby was silent. It was a very hard way of showing that she was sorry, she thought. She would rather have been shut up in her room, or go without pie or almost anything else that she could think of, instead of going away to boarding-school with Aunt Emma.

Much as she loved her aunt, she did not want to have to leave her father and mother for the sake of being with her. All at once a thought came into her head which made going away seem less hard. I am sure you will laugh when I tell you what it was that could console her in some part for the thought of leaving her father and mother. She remembered that once when she was upstairs in Mrs. Peterson's house, she saw a little trunk standing at the end of the wide hall, studded with brass-headed nails, and upon one end were the letters "M. D. K." She had asked Maude to whom the trunk belonged, and Maude had looked very important when she answered that it was her own trunk, and that the letters upon the end stood for Maude Delevan Birkenbaum. Ruby was wondering whether she should have a trunk like Maude's if she should go to boarding-school. It had seemed just the very nicest thing in the world to have a trunk of one's own with one's initials upon it in brass-headed nails, and she thought she could go, without being quite heart-broken, if only she had a trunk to take with her. Finally she said,—

"Papa, if I go to boarding-school, I shall have to have a trunk, won't I? And may it be a black trunk with my name on it in brass nails?"

Papa smiled, though Ruby did not see him.

"Yes, dear," he answered. "If you are a good little girl, and try not to worry your mother by fretting about going, and don't get into any more mischief before you go, I will certainly give you just such a trunk to take with you, if that will be any comfort to you."

"It certainly would be a comfort," Ruby answered, cuddling up closer to her papa. "And may I take some butternuts in it?"

"You will have to consult your Aunt Emma about what you shall put in it," her father answered, "but I will get you the trunk."

"And it will have a key?" asked Ruby.

"Yes, it will have a key," said her father. "Now, Ruby, mamma wants to see you a little while. Can I trust you to be a good little girl, and not disturb her when you go into her room? Her head aches very badly, and I only want you to stay in there long enough to kiss her and tell her how sorry you are for disturbing her so last night, and then you must go downstairs quietly. Will you remember?"

"Yes, papa," Ruby answered in subdued tones, and then she slipped down from his knee, and walked along the hall on tiptoe, and stole into her mother's room. When she saw her mother's pale face, and traces of tears on her cheeks, and knew that it was because she had been so naughty that the tears were there, Ruby wanted to bury her head in the pillow beside her mother, and have a good cry there; but she remembered what her father had told her, and kept very quiet. She only kissed her mother, and whispering how very sorry she was, she came away, feeling comforted and forgiven by her mother's kiss. "I don't see how I am ever bad to such a lovely mamma," she said to herself.

She was a little shy about going downstairs. It was not very pleasant to remember that the very first thing Aunt Emma had known about her when she came was that she was in mischief, and Ruby thought of course she would say something about it, and perhaps that Ann would reprove her, too.

But she was very pleasantly disappointed when at last she went into the sitting-room, where Aunt Emma was busy with some sewing.

She looked up and greeted her little niece as if she had not seen her before since her arrival; and she seemed so wholly unconscious of anything unusual in Ruby's not being down to breakfast, that the little girl thought perhaps her aunt had forgotten all about it. Ann did not say anything more to her about her naughtiness either, and before dinner-time Ruby was almost happy at the idea of going to boarding-school with a trunk, and a key, which she meant to wear upon a string around her neck.

She intended to persuade Ruthy to go, too, though. She was quite sure that not even the trunk could make her go away happily without her little friend.

CHAPTER VI.

PREPARATIONS.

Aunt Emma was very pleasant company for some time, but when she went upstairs to the sick-room, Ruby concluded that she would go over and see Ruthy.

She felt quite important as she walked along, thinking of the great news she had to tell. It did not take Ruby very long to forget about her troubles and penitences, and if it had not been for the sight of the blackened remains of the fire, and the pile of boards lying where her father had thrown them when he pushed them down and carried Ruby out, she might not have thought of last night's performance for some time.

As it was, she stopped the happy little song that had been on her lips, and walked along very quietly for a time, thinking how sorry she was that she had made her mother worse, and that she was going to be sent away from home because she could not be trusted.

While going to boarding-school might be a very great event, and an event which was quite unheard-of in the lives of any of Ruby's friends, yet she did not like to have to remember that it was partly as a punishment that she was going.

Before she reached Ruthy's, however, she had banished all unpleasant thoughts, and her one idea was to astonish Ruthy with the information that she was going to boarding-school, and was to have a trunk to take with her. She ran upon the porch calling,—

"Ruthy, Ruthy! Where are you?"

Mrs. Warren came to the door.

"Good-morning, Ruby," she said, looking gravely at the little girl. "How is your mamma this morning after her anxiety last night about you?"

Ruby had not thought that Mrs. Warren knew anything about her plan of playing Swiss Family Robinson, and her face grew very red, as she looked away from Mrs. Warren, and twisted the corner of her apron into a little point.

"How did you know?" she asked very faintly.

"Because your papa came over here looking for you, and then he drove back after a while to let us know that you were found, and were safe. I was very sorry to hear that you had frightened your mother so. How is she this morning?"

"She is worse this morning," and Ruby began to cry. It was so hard to have to tell Ruthy's mamma that she had made her own dear mother worse. "I did n't mean to make my mamma worse; I truly did n't, Mrs. Warren. I love my mamma just as much as Ruthy loves you, and maybe better, even if I do do things I ought n't to do. I never thought she would know about it, I truly didn't. If I had known that she would wake up and be frightened, I never would have gone out one step, even if I did think it would be fun."

Mrs. Warren led Ruby in and took her up in her lap.

"My dear little girl, if you would only stop and think before you get into mischief, I do not believe you would do half so many naughty things," she said. "I know you love your mother, but you think about Ruby first and what she wants to do, and forget to think about your mother until afterwards, and then it is too late to spare her anxiety about you. It would make her very unhappy if she knew how many things you do which, I am sure, you know she would not like."

"Indeed, I am going to try to be good," Ruby answered, wiping away her tears. "And I have a great secret, Mrs. Warren. At least, it is n't a secret exactly. It's somewhere that I am going, but I want to tell Ruthy first of all, and then I will tell you about it; and oh, I do hope you will let Ruthy go too. Will you?"

"I can't answer until I know where you are going," Mrs. Warren answered. "Does your papa know where you are going, Ruby?"

"Oh, yes, ma'am," Ruby answered promptly, glad that for once there was nothing wrong about her plan. "He told me about it this morning. It is only that I want Ruthy to know it the very first of all that I don't tell you about it this very minute, Mrs. Warren. You don't mind, do you?"

"Oh, no," Mrs. Warren replied. "If your papa knows about it, I am quite satisfied."

Ruby jumped down and went in search of Ruthy, who Mrs. Warren said was probably playing out in the barn.

"Ruthy! Ruthy!" called Ruby as she ran down and peeped in through the great doors. "Where are you, Ruthy?"

"Up in the hay loft," answered a smothered voice. "Come up here, Ruby."

So Ruby climbed up and found Ruthy curled up in a little nest of fragrant hay, with one of her favorite story-books.

"Oh, Ruby, tell me about last night," began Ruthy eagerly. "I was so frightened when it began to get dark, and I remembered that you were going to stay out-doors all alone by yourself; and I felt so bad that I almost cried. I could hardly go to sleep, I kept thinking about you so much. Did you go? Was n't it dreadful?"

Ruby was glad that Ruthy did not know how her papa had come over to find if Ruby was with Ruthy.

"Oh, yes," she answered. "I went out and stayed a long time, but it was n't very nice. Anyway, let's don't talk about that, Ruthy. I have got something to tell you that you could never, never guess, I don't believe, if you tried for one hundred times. Now I will give you six guesses, and you can see if you can guess right. I am going somewhere in about two weeks. Can you guess where?"

"Going somewhere?" echoed Ruthy. "Why, I don't believe I could possibly guess, Ruby. Let me think first."

She shut her eyes and tried to imagine where Ruby could be going, but she found it pretty hard work. Neither of the little girls had ever been away from home in their lives, farther than over to the grove where the Fourth-of-July picnics were always held, so it was not very strange that Ruthy could not think of any visit that Ruby would be likely to make. Perhaps Ruby was going to visit the grandmother who sometimes came to stay with Ruby's mamma for a few weeks, and who had sent the little girls their wonder balls when they learned to knit.

"I guess first that you are going to visit your grandma," she said.

"No," answered Ruby, triumphantly. "I just knew you could n't possibly guess right, but try again. I won't tell you until you have guessed six times."

"I am afraid I won't ever know, then," sighed Ruthy. "I can't think of six places to guess. Are you going to New York?"

"No," answered Ruby. "It is a great deal more important than going to New York. You know folks don't stay long when they go to New York, and they don't take a—" but she clapped her hands over her mouth to shut out the next word. "Dear me, I most told you the very most important part of the secret. I won't say another word for fear I will tell. Now guess again."

"I might as well ask you if you are going to the moon," Ruthy said.

"I truly can't guess once more, Ruby, so you will have to tell me."

"I am going to boarding-school," announced Ruby, triumphantly.

Ruthy was just as surprised as Ruby had expected her to be. She sat straight up in the hay, and let her book fall, while she looked at Ruby with wide-open eyes.

"What!" she exclaimed, as if she could not believe her ears. "Did you really say you were going to boarding-school, Ruby Harper?"

"Yes, I really am," Ruby responded, "but there 's more than that to tell you. What do you suppose I am going to have to take with me?"

"I am sure I don't know," Ruthy answered.

"I am going to have a trunk of my very own," said Ruby, proudly. "It will be like Maude Birkenbaum's, papa said it would be. It is to be black, and have a beautiful row of gold nails all around the top, and then at one end there will be 'M. D. B.' in letters made of the nails all driven in rows. Won't that be beautiful?"

"Yes, indeed," answered Ruthy. "But what will 'M. D. B.' stand for, Ruby?"

"Why, for my initials of course," Ruby answered. "Oh, no, I made a mistake. It won't be 'M. D. B.,' but 'R. T. H.,' to stand for Ruby Todd Harper. I forgot that my initials and Maude's were n't the same. But just think of it, Ruthy. To have a trunk of one's own and a key to it! I think that will be too lovely for anything."

"Are you glad you are going to boarding-school?" asked Ruthy, looking at her rather soberly.

"Why, yes, of course I am," said Ruby, trying to forget that it meant going away from home, too.

"How long will you stay, do you suppose?" asked Ruthy.

"Oh, I don't exactly know. Till mamma gets well again, papa said," Ruby replied. "I spose maybe about a year."

Ruby had rather vague ideas about the length of a year. She always counted a year from one Christmas to the next, or from one Fourth of July to the next, whichever happened to be nearest the time from which she was calculating; and though it seemed a long time when she looked back from one holiday to the last, yet she did not have a very good idea how much time it took for twelve months to pass away. Ruby knew her tables, and she could have told you in one minute, that it took three hundred and sixty-five days to make a year, but she did not know how long it took that procession of days to pass along and let the new year come in.

"Oh, dear," and Ruthy buried her face in the hay, and began to cry.

"Why, what is the matter?" asked Ruby, in surprise.

"I shall miss you so dreadfully," sobbed Ruthy. "I shall not have any one to play with, that is, any one like you, and I shall miss you all the time."

"But I am going to ask your mamma to let you go with me," Ruby said comfortingly. "I forgot to tell you, but I truly will. Do you suppose I would go away off to boarding-school without you, Ruthy Warren? You might know I would n't. Of course not. Come and let's go in now and ask your mother if you can't go with me."

But Ruthy cried harder than ever.

"But I don't want to go to boarding-school," she sobbed. "I want to stay with my mamma. I should just die if I went way off away from her. I don't want you to go either, Ruby. I don't see what you think it is nice to go to boarding-school for, anyway."

"Now, Ruthy, I thought you would go with me, even if you didn't think it would be very nice at first," Ruby said, in rather reproving tones. "Of course you think it would n't be nice, but it would be after you got used to it, and you would have a trunk, too, maybe. Wouldn't that be nice?"

But the trunk was no comfort to Ruthy. She could not understand how Ruby could bear to think of leaving her mother. She was quite sure she would never be willing to do it, and not Ruby's most eloquent representations to her of how delightful going away with a trunk would be, could induce her to want to accompany her.

"Oh, I wish you were not going, either," was all that Ruby could coax from her, after she had talked until she was tired.

CHAPTER VII.

MORE PREPARATIONS.

Thee was nothing that vain little Ruby enjoyed more than a sense of importance, and so she was quite happy for the next few days. All her little friends looked upon her with wonder when they heard that she was going away to boarding-school, and Ruby's announcement to them that she was going to take a trunk added to the importance of the occasion quite as much as she had hoped it would.

There was only a week in which to make all preparations for her going, so you can imagine that they were very busy days. Miss Abigail Hart, the dressmaker who made every one's clothes, when they were not made by people themselves, came to the house every day, and sewed all day long, and Aunt Emma helped her most of the time. If it had not been for the thoughts of the trunk, Ruby would have found some of these days very tiresome. She had to be always ready in case Miss Hart should want to try on any of her dresses, so she could not go very far away from the house, and she found Miss Hart's dressmaking very different from her mother's dressmaking.

Miss Abigail Hart was tall and thin, and as Ruby and many other little girls said, had quite forgotten all about the time when she was a little girl; so when she went to houses to sew, the children usually tried to keep out of her way as much as possible. Her hands were very cold, whether it was summer or winter, and she never liked it if any one whom she was fitting jumped about when her cold fingers touched one's neck. She wore long scissors, tied by a ribbon to her waist, and these scissors were always cold; and it was not at all a pleasant operation to have the waist of a dress fitted, and have Miss Abigail's cold fingers, and her still colder scissors creeping about one's neck.

"If you don't keep still it will not be my fault if you get a cut," Miss Abigail would say, and I am not sure but that some of the little girls were afraid that their very heads might be snipped off by a slip of those shining blades, if they wriggled about when the necks of their dresses were being trimmed down.

Miss Abigail was very slow, so it took a long time to go through this operation, and the worst part of it was that one fitting never was sufficient. At least twice, and sometimes three times she would repeat it, and there were plenty of Ruby's friends who had said that not for all the new dresses in the world would they want to have Miss Abigail fit them. They would rather have but one dress and have that dress made by their mothers, if they had to choose between that and those cold fingers and sharp scissors.

It was very pleasant to go to the store with Aunt Emma, and help choose the pretty calicoes and delaines which were to be made into dresses and help fill the little trunk. Ruby never felt more important than when she was perched upon the high stool before the counter and had four new dresses at once. She fancied that the store-keeper was more respectful in his tone than he usually was when he addressed little girls, and that he was much impressed by the fact that Aunt Emma let her select the pattern herself instead of choosing for her.

The calicoes were very pretty. One was covered with little rosebuds upon a cream-tinted ground, and the other had little dark-blue moons upon a light-blue ground. The delaines were brown and blue; and then besides these dresses, Ruby's best cashmere was to be let down, and have the sleeves lengthened, so that it would still be nice for a best dress.

Ruby had never had so many new dresses all at once in her life before, and she felt very important when her papa brought them home in the buggy, and they were all spread out before Miss Abigail.

Miss Abigail looked at them very wisely, with her head a little upon one side. She rubbed them between her fingers, wondered whether they would wash well, and finally looked at Ruby, and said,—

"I trust you are a very thankful little girl for all the mercies you have. So you know that there are some poor little children who have but rags to wear?"

"Yes 'm," said Ruby, meekly.

"Then don't you think you ought to appreciate all the blessings that have been bestowed upon you?"

"Yes 'm," Ruby replied again.

"Then you must try to be an obedient, gentle child, and do as you are bid in everything."

"Yes 'm," said Ruby, wishing in the bottom of her heart that the dresses were all made.

She had never had very much to do with Miss Abigail herself, although she had often seen her, and two or three times she had spent a day at the house, helping Mrs. Harper make one of her own dresses. Upon those occasions, however, Ruby had spent the day with Ruthy, and so she had only been with Miss Abigail a little while in the morning, and had not had much to say to her.

"If Miss Abigail was my mamma, I would not stay in the same house with her," Ruby said to herself. "I guess that is why she has n't any little girls,— because she don't know how to make them happy. I don't want to be told all the time about being good, I guess."

But Ruby had to listen to a great many lectures, whether she liked them or not, in the next few days. Miss Abigail came and stayed with them for all the rest of the week, and as she believed in little girls being made useful, Ruby had to spend a good deal of time in picking out bastings, and doing other little things for Miss Abigail.

"Oh, dear, I have n't done one single thing since I can remember," Ruby said, impatiently, to Ruthy one day when her little friend came over to see her; "I have n't done one single thing but pick out bastings and have Miss Abigail telling me how good I ought to be 'cause I have so many new dresses. I do wish she was all done and had gone away."

"But then you will go away, too, you know," Ruthy suggested.

"I wish I would n't; I wish I was going to stay here for a week after she went," Ruby answered. "I think Aunt Emma might stop her, I do so."

"How do you mean?" asked Ruthy.

"Well, I know what I would do," said Ruby. "I would say to her this way—" and Ruby held her head very high, and tried to look exceedingly dignified—"I should say, 'Miss Abigail, if you will please tend to making Ruby's dresses, I will tend to her behavior.'"

Ruthy looked rather shocked.

"I am afraid that would make Miss Abigail feel dreadfully bad, to have your auntie say such a thing," she said. "I think Miss Abigail is real nice, I truly do. She saves pretty pieces of calico for my patch-work, and once she gave me a sash for my doll; don't you remember it?—that blue one, with a little rose bud in the middle."

"Well, I don't like her," and Ruby shook her shoulders. "And I don't think it's nice in you to like her, when she makes me perfectly miserable. How would you like it if every time you wanted to do anything you heard her calling you, and had to go in and be fitted and fitted. She holds pins in her mouth, too, a whole row of them, and mamma never lets me do that, so Miss Abigail ought not to, and I just think I will tell her so. She has a whole row of them, just as long as her mouth is wide, and they bristle straight out when she talks. Just suppose she should drop some down my neck when she is talking. They would stick in to me, and hurt me like everything before I could get them out. I guess I would n't like that, would I? And if you had to stand just hours and hours, and have her cold fingers poking around your neck, and those great sharp scissors going snip, snip all around your neck, just where they would cut great pieces out if you dared move, I don't believe you would like that yourself, Ruthy Warren, even if she did give you things for your doll."

"No, I don't s'pose I would like it any better than you do," assented Ruthy, who was determined not to quarrel with her little friend, when they were so soon to be separated.

"Ruby, Miss Abigail wants you," called Aunt Emma.

Ruby made a wry face.

"There she is again," she exclaimed. "It's just the way the whole livelong time. I think if she knew how to make dresses, she ought not to have to fit so much. If I fitted my doll so often when I made her a dress, I guess her head would fall off. It would get shaky anyway, with so much fussing. Wait till I come back, Ruthy, and then we will play."

Miss Abigail was waiting to fit Ruby's blue delaine, and it looked so pretty that Ruby forgot how unwilling she had been to come in and have it fitted.

She showed her pleasure in it so plainly that good Miss Abigail was afraid that the little girl was in danger of becoming vain, and thought it best to warn her against this state of mind.

"I am afraid it is n't the best thing for you, Ruby Warren, to have so many new clothes all at once," she said, with the row of pins waving up and down, as she spoke through her teeth, which she did not open when she spoke, lest the pins should fall out. "If any one thinks more of clothes than they should, then dress is a snare and a temptation to them, and I am much afraid that that is what it is going to be to you. Better for you to have only one dress to your back than to put clothes in the wrong place in your mind, and let them make you vain and conceited. What are clothes, anyway? There is n't any thing to be so proud of in them. Now this nice wool delaine was once growing on a sheep's back. Do you suppose that sheep was vain because it was covered with wool? No, it never thought anything about it. And so you see that you ought n't to be proud of it either."

"I think new dresses are very nice," said Ruby, speaking cautiously, lest she should inadvertently turn her head, and the sharp points of the scissors should run into her neck.

Miss Abigail felt that she must say still more, for it was evident that Ruby was putting too much value upon her dress.

"But it is n't new," she said.

"Oh, Miss Abigail, it truly is," exclaimed Ruby, forgetting herself and turning her head so suddenly that if the scissors had been in the right place, the points would surely have run into her. Fortunately, Miss Abigail had stopped to see how the neck looked, and her scissors were hanging by her side for a moment. "Why, of course, it is new. I went with Aunt Emma to the store, and helped buy it my very own self, so I know it is brand-new. Why, I should think you could tell it is new, it is so pretty and bright, and there is n't one single teenty tonty wrinkle in it."

"Yes, it is new to you," Miss Abigail answered solemnly. "But when you think about the matter, Ruby Harper, you know that the sheep wore it first, and you only have it second-hand, as you might say. Now, I should think a little girl was very silly that thought herself better than any one else, and let her thoughts rest on her clothes because she wore a sheep's old suit of wool made up in a little different way. Shall I tell you some verses that my mother made me learn when I was a little girl, because I was proud of a new pelisse?"

"Yes 'm," said Ruby, meekly, taking a great deal of pleasure in the thought that when Miss Abigail was a little girl she had been naughty sometimes, and had had to learn verses as a punishment.

> "'How proud we are, how fond to show
>
> Our clothes, and call them rich and new,
>
> When the poor sheep and silk-worm wore
>
> That very clothing long before.
>
> "'The tulip and the butterfly
>
> Appear in gayer coats than I;
>
> Let me be dressed fine as I will,
>
> Flies, worms, and flowers exceed me still.'"

"I don't think worms look nicer than I do," said Ruby, not very politely, when Miss Abigail had finished. "And I am very sorry for you, Miss Abigail, if you had to learn such ugly verses. If you had had a mamma like mine you would have had a better time, I think."

Miss Abigail looked severely over her brass-bowed spectacles at Ruby, almost too shocked to speak for a moment.

"I am sure, I don't know what your mother would say, Ruby Harper, if she heard you talking that way. I am sure she would think that you were no credit to her bringing-up. You have a good mother, one of the best mothers that ever lived, and your father is such a good man, too, that I am sure I don't see where you get your pert ways from. I was a happy child, because I was, in the main, a good child, and no one ever had a better mother than mine; and I have tried to follow the way in which I was brought up, if I do say it myself. Those were counted to be very pretty verses when I was a child, and I don't know but they were better than to-day. At any rate, in my day, children were taught to have a little respect for their elders, and there are very few that do that now. There were some other verses that I was going to tell a good deal of the nonsense that children learn you, but if that is your opinion of those I did tell you, there is no use in my taking so much trouble."

Miss Abigail looked sorrowful as well as vexed, and Ruby wished that she had not told her what she thought of the verses.

"I suppose she thinks they are nice," she said to herself; "and mamma would be sorry if she thought I had been rude to Miss Abigail."

Ruby was going away from her mother so soon that her conscience was more tender than usual, and she did not want to do what she knew her mother would not like.

"Please tell me the other verses, Miss Abigail," she said. "I did not know you liked those other verses, or I would not have called them ugly."

"I am glad you did not mean to be a rude child," said Miss Abigail, pleased by Ruby's apology. "Your mother takes so much pains with you that it would be a pity for you not to be a good child. Yes, I will tell you the others, and while I am repeating them you can sit down upon this little ottoman, and pick out the bastings in this sleeve."

While Ruby pulled the basting-thread out, and wound it on a spool as Miss Abigail had taught her, half wishing that she had not said anything about the other verses, since she might now have been out at play with Ruthy, Miss Abigail repeated some more of the verses she had learned when she, too, was a little girl like Ruby:—

"'Come, come, Mister Peacock, you must not be proud,

Although you can boast such a train;

For many a bird, far more highly endowed,

Is not half so conceited nor vain.

Let me tell you, gay bird, that a suit of fine clothes

Is a sorry distinction at most,

And seldom much valued, excepting by those

Who only such graces can boast.

The nightingale certainly wears a plain coat,

But she cheers and delights with her song;

While you, though so vain, cannot utter a note,

To please by the use of your tongue.

The hawk cannot boast of a plumage so gay,

But piercing and clear is her eye;

And while you are strutting about all the day,

She gallantly soars in the sky.

The dove may be clad in a plainer attire,

But she is not selfish and cold;

And her love and affection more pleasure impart

Than all your fine purple and gold.

So you see, Mister Peacock, you must not be proud,

Although you can boast such a train;

For many a bird is more highly endowed,

And not half so conceited and vain.'"

"I think I like that ever so much better," said Ruby, jumping up as Miss Abigail finished, and handing back the sleeve, from which she had pulled all the basting-threads.

"Now can I go over to Ruthy's, Miss Abigail? Aunt Emma told me that I must ask you before I went away anywhere, for fear you would want me."

"No, I shall not want you any more until nearly tea-time," Miss Abigail answered, as she scrutinized the sleeve to see whether Ruby had left any bastings in it. "Now remember what I have told you, Ruby, child, about setting your heart upon your fine clothes. Clothes do not make people, and if you are not a well-behaved child, polite and respectful to your betters, it will not make any difference to any one how well you may be dressed."

"Yes 'm," Ruby answered, as she ran away to find Ruthy, thinking that little girls in Miss Abigail's time must have been very different from the little girls she knew, and wondering whether Miss Abigail looked as tall and thin when she was a little girl as she did now, and whether she used to be just as proper and precise.

It was so funny to think of Miss Abigail as a little girl that Ruby laughed aloud at the thought, as she looked for her little friend. She was quite sure of one thing: if she had been a little girl when Miss Abigail was a little girl, she would not have chosen her for a friend. Ruthy was the only little girl in all the world that she could wish to have always for a friend, for who else would be always willing to give up her own way, and yield so patiently to impetuous little Ruby in everything.

CHAPTER VIII.

READY.

Ruby thoroughly enjoyed all the preparations that were being made for her departure. Every day, and a great many times a day, the little trunk would be opened and something more put into its hungry mouth, and it was soon quite full of the things which Ruby was to take with her. Of course she did not get into mischief during these busy days,—there was no time for it. It was only when Ruby had nothing else to think about that she devised plans for mischief. At last everything was ready the evening before she was to start. Miss Abigail had finished all that she had to do; she had bidden Ruby good-by, with a long lecture upon how she ought to behave when she was at school, so as to set a good example to her school-mates, and reflect credit upon her father and mother and the training they had given her, and then she had concluded by giving Ruby something that I am afraid she valued much more than the advice,—a pretty little house-wife, of red silk, which she had made for her, with everything in it that Ruby would need if she wanted to take any stitches.

When Ruby saw it she was sorry that she had twisted about so much, and showed so plainly how impatient she was growing of the long talk which preceded it.

Then Miss Abigail had tied on her large black bonnet, and Ruby had watched her going down the road with a sense of relief that there would be no more fitting of dresses, with cold fingers and still colder scissors, and no more lectures upon good behavior. However, she was so pleased and surprised by the pretty gift that she felt more kindly towards Miss Abigail than she would have believed it possible.

Ruby's old dresses had been made over until they looked just like new ones, and the last stitches had been taken in her new ones, and little white ruffles were basted in the necks, so that they were all ready to put on. Everything had been carefully folded up and packed in her trunk,—not only her clothes, but the little farewell gifts that her friends had brought her.

She had a nice pencil-box, filled with pencils and pen-holders, two penwipers, as well as a box of the dearest little note-paper, just the right size for her to write upon, with her initial "R" at the top of the paper.

Orpah had brought her a mysterious box, carefully tied up in paper, which she had made Ruby promise that she would not open until she unpacked her trunk at school; so that gave Ruby something nice to look forward to when she should reach her journey's end.

Ruby had fully intended to take her kitten with her, and she was very much disappointed when Aunt Emma told her that that was one of the things she would have to leave behind her.

Ann promised to take the very best care of Tipsey, and that promise comforted Ruby somewhat, although she still wished that she might take her pet with her.

It was not until the last evening came that Ruby fully realized that she was going away to leave her papa and mamma the next day. Then she felt as if she would gladly give up her trunk and all her new clothes and everything that she had been enjoying so much, if she might only stay at home.

For the first time her promise to her father to be brave about going away cost her a great effort. Her mother had not been nearly so well since the night she had been so anxious about her little girl, and Ruby knew that she must not worry her by crying or fretting about going away.

But she climbed up on her father's lap after she had eaten her supper, and put her head down upon his broad shoulder, with the feeling that nothing in all the wide world could make up to her for being away from him and from her dear mother.

She wished with all her heart that she had tried to be a good girl during her mother's illness, for then it would not have been necessary to send her away to school. But now it was too late, for everything was all ready for her going, and Ruby was quite sure that coax and tease as hard as she might, her father would not change his plans.

"I don't want to go away, papa," she said, with a little sob in her voice, as Tipsey scrambled up in her lap, and curling herself into a little round ball of fur began to purr a soft little tune.

"Don't you want to leave Tipsey?" asked her father, playfully.

"It is n't only Tipsey," said Ruby, while a big tear splashed down upon her father's hand. "It is you and mamma, most of all, and Ruthy, and everybody. I know I shall not be one single bit happy at school when I can't come home and see you when I want to, and I shall just most die, I am sure I shall."

"Little daughter, we both love mother, don't we?" asked her father, stroking Ruby's dark hair gently.

"Yes, sir," answered Ruby, with a tremulous voice.

"And we would do anything to help her get well again?"

"Why, of course," Ruby answered again.

"Then we must do some things that are hard, if we really want to help her. You know how sick she has been the last few days. I don't want you to feel as if I was sending you away only as a punishment for running away that night. Perhaps if you had not done that particular thing, I might not have given my consent to this plan, but I am sure you are enough of a little woman to see what a help it will be to mother. If she is to get well again, she needs to have her mind kept perfectly free from worry; and when you are running about with no one to take care of you except Ann, who is too busy to do much for you, she is worrying all the time for fear something may happen to you, or that you may get into some mischief. Now if she knows you are safe at school with Aunt Emma, where you will be well taken care of, and will study your lessons, and try to be good and obedient, then she will feel so much happier about you that it will do more toward helping her to get well than all the medicine in the world. There are some things that I can do for her. I can take care of her, and give her medicine, and see that nothing troubles her in the house, but there is something for you to do that I cannot do. This is to be your share of helping dear mother get well. If you go away bravely, and try to study and be a good girl, so that Aunt Emma can write home in each letter that you are doing just as mother would wish you to do, you will be helping her even more than I will. If you think only about yourself, you will cry about going, and fret to come home, until mother will be troubled about you, and perhaps think it best for you to come home again; but if you think about mother, you will be my own brave little daughter, and then mother will soon be well again, and we will send for our little Ruby, and she will come home wiser and better-behaved than when she went away, and we will all be so happy. I am sure I know which you are going to do."

"I am going to be just as brave as can be," Ruby answered, winking back the tears which had been trying to roll down her cheeks, and rubbing out of sight the great shining one which had splashed down upon Tipsey's soft fur. "Yes, papa, I am going to be just as brave as anything. I won't cry. I won't say one word about wanting to come home in my letters, and I will study so hard that I shall stay up at the head of the class just as I do here, and the teacher will think I am ever so—"

"Be careful, darling," interrupted her father. "I don't want my little girl to think so much of herself. If you go to school thinking that you are going to be so much more clever than all the other little girls, I am afraid you will find out that you are sadly mistaken, and then you will be very unhappy. Don't think of excelling the other girls, but think of doing the very best you can because it is right, and because it will make mother and father happy. I would rather have my little Ruby at the very foot of the class, and have her unselfish and gentle, than have her at the head, with a proud and unlovely spirit. Of course I should be very glad to have my little daughter excel in her lessons, for then I should know that she was studying and trying to improve herself as much as possible, but I don't want to have her as vain as a little peacock over it. And you know, Ruby, that it is generally when you are trusting in yourself that you do something that you are the most sorry for. Pride goes before a fall, you remember."

"I will try not to be proud," said Ruby, penitently. "But you don't know how I like to be praised, papa. It scares Ruthy, and she does n't like it one bit, but I like it from my head down to my feet, I truly do. I like to have people say I am ever so smart, and I don't see how I can help it."

"By trying to forget yourself, dear, and keeping self in the back-ground as much as you can in everything that you do. When you are trying to do anything well, remember that it is only just what you ought to do. God has given you a good memory, and a readiness to learn, and so you ought to do the very best with the powers he has given you. You have no more reason to be vain of them than a peacock has to be vain of his fine tail. And it is better to be lovable than clever, and any one who is conceited never makes the friends that a modest child does. Now promise me that you will try, little daughter, to be gentle and modest, and not come back to us selfish and full of conceit."

"I will truly try, papa," Ruby answered. "That is harder for me to try than to try to learn my lessons or to keep the rules, but I will truly try, and you shall see how brave I will be in the morning when I go away. Why, papa, I am brave this very minute. I could just cry and cry, it makes me feel so full to think that this time to-morrow night you will be here just the same, and I will be ever so far away."

"We will think about the time when you will come home again," said her father, quickly, for Ruby's voice sounded very much as if a word more would bring the tears. "Some day I shall drive down to the station and a young lady with a trunk will get off the cars, and I shall hardly know who it is, you will have grown so fast. Little girls always grow fast when they go to boarding-school, you know."

"Do they?" asked Ruby, eagerly. "Oh, papa, do you s'pose I can have long dresses next year?"

"Why, then people would think you were a little baby again," said her papa, pretending to misunderstand her. "They would say, 'Why, Ruby Harper wore long dresses when she was six months old, and now she has them on again. She must have grown backwards.'"

"Now, papa Harper, you are making fun of me," exclaimed Ruby. "I mean long dresses like young ladies wear. I want to be grown up. Will I be big enough to wear dresses with a train next year if I grow fast."

"If you should grow fast enough," her father answered, pinching her cheek, "but I don't think you will do that, Ruby. You would have to grow like Jack's beanstalk, if you expect to spring up into a young lady in a year. Why, then I would not have any little girl, and what would I do for some one to hold in my lap?"

"Oh, I guess I don't want to grow too big to sit in lap," Ruby answered, nestling closer to her father. "I forgot that part of it. I will wait for ever so many years for long dresses, if I must give up sitting in lap. Well, I will grow as fast as I can, but not so fast that I won't be your little Ruby any longer."

"And now, dear, say good-night to mamma and go to bed," said her father, as he heard the clock striking. "We will have to be up bright and early in the morning, and I want you to have a good sleep."

By the time the stars were looking down Ruby was sound asleep in her little trundle-bed for the last time for many weeks.

CHAPTER IX.

THE JOURNEY.

Ruby and Aunt Emma were to start at nine o'clock, and as there were a great many little things to be done before the travellers should get off, the whole house was astir very early in the morning. Ruby was very much excited over her journey, but there was a little lump that kept arising in her throat all the time as if it would choke her if she did not swallow it back.

Ruthy was to go over to the station with her, and see her off, and it was hardly daybreak when she came over to Ruby's house, eager to have as long a time as possible with her little friend before she should go away.

Ruby felt as if she was a little queen, every one was so kind to her, and so anxious to please her in every way. Even Ann was wonderfully subdued, and when Ruby came downstairs, took her in her arms and said: "I don't know what we shall do without the precious child, I am sure." Coming from Ann, this was indeed a great compliment, and Ruby felt as if Ann was really very nice, indeed, since she had so high an opinion of the little girl.

"Are n't you sorry you have been so cross to me, sometimes?" asked Ruby, presently, thinking that if Ann would admit that she had said a great deal that she did not mean in the past, she would feel still happier.

Ann was sorry to have the child from whom she had never been separated for a whole day, go away for weeks, but she was not by any means disposed to admit that Ruby had not deserved all the scoldings she had over given her, and her voice had quite a little of its usual sharpness as she answered,—

"You know as well as I do, Ruby Harper, that you 've been enough to try the patience of a saint many and many a time, more particularly since your mother has been taken ill, and though I 'm sorry you 're going away, I am sure it is the best thing for you, for you had got long past my managing, and nobody knew what you were going to do next. If you were n't going to school, likely enough you would burn us all down in our beds some night."

Ruby looked rather crestfallen.

"I don't think you need be cross the very last thing when I am going away so far, and you won't see me for ever and ever so long again," she said, with a little quiver in her voice.

"Well, I did n't mean to be," said Ann, giving her another hug. "It's only that I got provoked that I said that. You see you and me have a lot to learn yet, Ruby, before we can say and do just what we ought to, and nothing else. I'll take it all back, and I'll show you the nice cake I have made for your lunch on the cars."

Ruby followed Ann to the buttery, and admired the cake with its white crust of icing, that looked like a coating of frost, to Ann's content, and would have been quite willing to have had a piece of it then and there, if Ann would have permitted it.

Everybody talked a great deal about everything but Ruby's going away, for nobody wanted to give the little girl time enough to think about it, lest she should grow homesick; and it seemed quite like a party, Ruby thought, as she sat beside her father at the table, with Ruthy sitting by her, all ready for another breakfast, she had risen so early.

After breakfast papa went down to the stable to harness up; the little trunk was shut for the last time, and the key turned and put in Aunt Emma's pocket-book,—greatly to Ruby's disappointment, for she wanted to keep it herself; but Aunt Emma said she might have it after they got safely to school, but it would be very inconvenient if she should lose it on the way there, and she tried to console herself with that promise. Ruby had had a parting frolic with Tipsey, and Ruthy had promised to come over and play with the kitten very often, so that she would not miss her little mistress too much, and now Ruby was going to say good-by to her mother, and have a few quiet minutes with her, before it should be time to put her hat and jacket on.

The room was dark and quiet, and when Ruby went in, old Mrs. Maggs, who spent all her time in staying with sick people and nursing them, got up and went out, so that the little girl should have her mother all to herself.

Ruby cuddled her face down beside her dear mother's face, in the pillow, and it was all the little girl could do to keep from bursting into tears, and begging that she might not be sent away. She remembered her promise to her father to be brave, and she swallowed the lump in her throat, back, over and over again, while her mother told her how she hoped that her little daughter would be a good girl, so that all she should hear from Aunt Emma would be good news, of Ruby's improvement in her studies, and of her good conduct.

Ruby listened to every word, and she promised her mother very earnestly that she would indeed try to conquer her self-will, and be good.

"That will help you get well, won't it, mamma?" she asked, stroking the white face tenderly.

"Yes, darling, nothing will help me get well faster than that," her mother answered, giving her a tender kiss.

It was very hard to say good-by when papa's voice called,—

"Come little daughter, the carriage is ready." It was harder than Ruby had had any idea that it would be. It seemed as if she could not possibly say good-by to her mother, and go out of the room, knowing that she could not kiss her good-night or good-morning any more for weeks and weeks. If it had been any one else, but to go away from her seemed quite impossible.

"Good-by, darling. Remember you are going to help me get well again," her mother said, drawing the little girl's face down for a last kiss, and that helped Ruby to be very brave. She kissed her mother over and over again, and then jumped up and went out of the room without one word.

The lump in her throat was growing so big that she knew she should cry in a moment if she did not hurry away.

"I was brave, papa, I was brave," she said, when she went out into the hall and found her father waiting for her; but the tears came then fast and thick for a moment.

"Now you will be my brave little daughter again, I know," said her father, comfortingly, "for it is time for us to start now. I am afraid the train would not wait for us if you were not at the station in time, and it would never do to miss the train on your first journey, would it?"

Ruby smiled through her tears.

"Don't you think they would wait when they saw the trunk on the platform, papa? I should think they would know somebody was going away then, and would wait."

"No, I don't think that even for anything as important as the trunk, the train would wait," her father answered.

Ann helped Ruby put on her hat and jacket with unusual gentleness, and Ruby thought that Ann looked very much as if she wanted to cry.

"Do you feel sorry, really, that I am going away, Ann?" she asked.

"Of course I do, honey," Ann answered.

All at once Ruby remembered how she had teased Ann, how many times she had been rude to her, and had done what she knew Ann did not want her to, and she put her arms around Ann's neck.

"Ann, I 'm sorry I have been so bad," she whispered. "I will be good when I come home again."

Ann was very much touched by Ruby's apology.

"Never you think about that," she answered. "I'll miss you dreadfully, and I shall never remember anything but the times you have been as good as a little lamb; so you need n't worry your head about that."

"Time to start," called papa again; so Ruby climbed up in the front seat, where she was to sit with her father, and Aunt Emma and Ruthy got in behind her. The little trunk, with Ruby's initials upon it, had already been taken down to the station, and was waiting for her there. It was quite a little drive to the station, and they had not started any too soon, for by the time papa had purchased the tickets, and had given Ruby the little pocket-book, that he had saved for a parting surprise, with a crisp ten-cent bill in it, some bright pennies, and in an inside compartment what seemed to Ruby like untold wealth, a whole dollar note, the distant whistle of the train was heard. And then almost before Ruby knew it she had said good-by to Ruthy, who could not keep her tears back when she said good-by to her little friend, and she was sitting by the window, where she could look out at Ruthy, when the train started, and her papa leaned over to give her a last kiss and hug.

"Good-by. God bless and keep my little daughter," he said tenderly.

The engine shrieked and whistled, the bell rang, and then with a jerk the train began to move, and Ruby looked out, with her face pressed close to the window, to see her father just as long as she possibly could. He was on the platform by Ruthy now, and he waved his handkerchief as the train started, and threw kisses to his little girl. Ruby pressed her face closer and closer against the glass, but at last it was of no use. There was only an indistinct blur where papa and Ruthy had been standing, for Ruby's eyes were so full of tears that she could not see them, and by the time she had taken out her new handkerchief and wiped them away, the train had begun to go so fast that she could not see the station at all. It was far behind her, and Ruby had really begun her first journey.

It was hard work not to put her head down in Aunt Emma's lap and cry as much as she wanted to, but Ruby glanced about the car, and saw that every one else was looking very happy, and watching the things that passed by the windows, so she thought, with some pride, that if she should cry people might not know that it was because she was going away from her dear papa and mamma and Ruthy, but they might think that she was frightened because she had never been in the cars before, and she certainly did not want them to know that.

She wiped the tears away from her eyes and sat up very straight, looking out of the window as if she was very much interested in everything she saw. Really, she could not have told you one thing that they went past. She was fighting back the tears, and her longing to have the train stopped and get off even now, and go back home again, where every one loved her so much; and it took all her courage and resolution not to break down.

Aunt Emma guessed what the little girl was thinking about, and she did not disturb her for a little while, until she thought that Ruby could talk without letting the tears come.

Then, all at once, she began to talk about the places they would pass on their way to school, and Ruby grew so interested in listening to her that the lump in her throat went away, and she really began to enjoy the journey.

She looked about the car at the other passengers, and she wondered whether they all knew that she was going away to school and had a little trunk of her very own. It seemed to Ruby as if it was such an important occasion that somehow every one must know, even if they had not been told about it.

It was very pleasant to travel, she decided, after a little while, and she wondered why it was that when she looked out of the window, it seemed as if everything was running past the train, instead of the train seeming to be in motion. It was very funny, and Ruby almost laughed when they passed a field full of cows, which shot by the window as if they had been running with all their might, when really they had been standing quite still, looking with soft, wondering eyes at the noisy monster that shrieked and whistled as it rushed on its way, drawing a long train of cars after it.

CHAPTER X.

MAKING FRIENDS.

By and by a man dressed in blue clothes with brass buttons came through the car, stopping at each seat and looking at people's tickets.

"That is the conductor, and he wants to look at the tickets," said Aunt Emma. "Would you like to give him the tickets, Ruby?"

Of course Ruby wanted to do this, and she changed places with Aunt Emma, and sat at the end of the seat, waiting for the conductor to come.

She felt very grown-up and important as she handed the little pieces of pasteboard to him, and wondered whether he would think that she was taking her Aunt Emma on a journey because she had the tickets; but the conductor rather disappointed her. He did not seem to be at all surprised that a little girl should give him the tickets, but he took them and after looking at them for a moment, punched a little hole in them.

This did not please Ruby at all. She had not noticed that he had done this same thing to every one else's ticket, and she exclaimed,—

"Please don't do that, you will spoil those tickets, and they are all we have got."

The conductor smiled, and so did several other people who had heard Ruby's speech.

"I have n't spoiled the tickets, sissy," the conductor said good-naturedly.

When he went on to the next seat Ruby showed the tickets to her Aunt Emma.

"He says he did not spoil them, but I just think he did," she whispered. "I think it spoils tickets to have a hole made in them, don't you, Aunt Emma? Now spose they are not good any more, how shall we get to school? Will they put us off the cars?"

"The tickets will be all right, Ruby," Aunt Emma answered smilingly. "Now put them back in my pocket-book again, so that they will not get lost, and by and by another conductor will get on the train and will want to see them, and then you shall show them to him."

"Will he make another hole in them?" asked Ruby, who still felt as if the tickets would be much nicer without the little hole in them.

"Yes, there will be three more holes made in them before we give them up," Aunt Emma answered.

"Give them up?" echoed Ruby. "What do you mean, Aunt Emma? We don't give them to any body, do we?"

"Yes, just before we get off the cars the conductor will take them."

"It seems pretty dreadful to spend so much money for tickets and then not be allowed to keep them," Ruby said. "Don't you think he would let me keep mine just to remember the journey by, if I should ask him?"

"No, he could not do that," Aunt Emma answered. "You will have to give yours up just as every one else will. But you have had a long ride for the ticket, you know, Ruby, so you must not feel as if your ticket had been taken away and you had received nothing in exchange."

"Oh, I forgot that," Ruby answered, and then she leaned her face against the window and looked out again at the places they were passing. By and by the old gentleman in the seat in front of Ruby looked around and when he saw the little girl, he smiled at her with a pair of very kind blue eyes, and said,—

"Little girl, don't you want to come in here and visit me a little while?"

Ruby was very willing to do this, for she was tired of looking out of the window, and Aunt Emma had a headache and did not feel like talking; so in a minute she had slipped past her aunt, and was in the next seat, very willing to be entertained.

The old gentleman was very fond of little girls, and as he had a whole host of grandchildren, he knew just what little girls and boys liked. He told Ruby some funny stories about the way people had to travel before steam cars were in use, and then he told her about the first school he ever went to, and how he had to go all alone, and had a pretty hard time with the older boys, who were very fond of teasing younger ones.

Ruby was very much interested, and told him in return that she, too, was going to school for the first time.

By and by a boy came through the cars with a basket on his arm.

"Oranges, apples, bananas, pears," he called out, and the old gentleman beckoned to him.

"Come here, and let this little lady choose what she would like to have," he said; and the boy brought the basket to Ruby, and rested it upon the arm of the seat, while she looked into it.

The old gentleman was very, very nice, she thought, for he not only knew how to be so entertaining, but he called Ruby "a little lady," and if there was one thing in all the world that Ruby liked better than another it was to be considered grown-up, and to be spoken of as a little lady.

The old gypsy woman had called her a little lady, though Ruby did not like to remember her, but it was quite proper that a little girl who was going to boarding-school should be considered grown-up, even if she did not have long dresses on.

"What will you have, my dear?" asked the old gentleman. "Will you have an orange or a banana, or is there something else you would prefer?"

A large yellow Bartlett pear attracted Ruby's eyes.

"I think I would like this," she answered.

"Very well, my dear," he said. "Now as my eyes are not very good, would you be kind enough to take some money out of my pocketbook and pay the boy?"

This was even still more delightful, and Ruby felt as if long dresses could not make her feel one inch more grown-up than she felt when she opened the big purse with its brass clasps, took out some money, and paid the boy, receiving some pennies in change which she dropped back into the purse again.

"I see you are quite used to making purchases," said the old gentleman, with a funny little twinkle in his eye, as he watched the happy little face beside him.

"I don't very often buy anything and pay the money for it," Ruby said truthfully. "That is, except at the store, and that don't seem to count because mamma always gives me just the right money, all wrapped up so I won't lose it. But I think it is very nice to buy things. Didn't you want a pear, too, sir?"

"No, thank you," answered the old gentleman. "Now would you like to have me fix the pear so you can eat it without getting any juice upon your pretty dress?"

"Yes, please," Ruby answered, so he spread a newspaper upon his lap, and taking out his knife, cut the pear into quarters, and proceeded to peel it, and cut it into nice little pieces, just the right size to eat.

Ruby watched him with a great deal of interest. She liked him more and more all the time, and she was quite sure that it would be very nice to be one of his grandchildren, of whom he had told her.

It had been some time now since Ruby and Aunt Emma had started upon their journey, and when Aunt Emma saw what the old gentleman was doing she leaned forward and offered Ruby the lunch-basket.

"It would be very nice for you to eat your lunch now, if you are hungry," she said. "Suppose you eat a sandwich first, and then the pear, and some cake afterwards. You can offer the basket to your friend, and perhaps he would like a sandwich, too."

Ruby was very much pleased to find that the old gentleman thought that this would be a very good plan, and that he was glad of a sandwich, so the party had quite a little picnic together. Aunt Emma ate her lunch too, and Ruby spread the white napkin that was in the top of the lunch-box over her lap, and laid the sandwiches out upon it, so that the old gentleman might help himself.

The pear was such a big one that Ruby could divide it both with the old gentleman and with Aunt Emma and still have plenty for herself, and some time passed very pleasantly in eating the lunch, and putting what was left carefully back into the box again.

By this time Ruby had begun to be very tired of riding in the cars. She did not want to look out of the window any more, and she began to feel a little homesick. She grew very quiet, as she began to wonder what Ruthy was doing just now. The old gentleman had told her that it was eleven o'clock, so she knew that Ruthy was probably having a nice game at recess with the other children. This was the first day of school at home, and Ruby remembered how she had always enjoyed that first day. It was so pleasant to put everything to rights in her desk just as she meant to have it all the year, to have her old seat by Ruthy where she had sat ever since she first began to go to school, and to look at the new scholars, and wonder whether she would have much trouble in keeping at the head of the class.

The old gentleman wondered what made his little companion so quiet, and looking down at her, he saw the tears beginning to gather in her eyes. He guessed a little of what she was thinking about. Of course he could not know all about school, and about Ruthy, but he knew she was thinking about some one at home.

He looked back, and saw that Aunt Emma had put her head down upon the back of the seat, and with a handkerchief over her face was trying to take a little nap in the hope that it would help her aching head. He wondered what he could do to keep Ruby from becoming homesick and tired.

"Let me tell you about one of my little grandchildren," he said, and Ruby winked the tears away and looked up at him. "She is a little girl just about your age, and sometimes when we go on a journey together, as we often do,—for every year I go and get her, and bring her to stay with me for two or three weeks in the summer time,—she gets tired of riding in the cars so long at once, and what do you suppose she does?"

"What does she do?" asked Ruby.

"She reaches into my pocket,—this outside pocket, here,—and takes out this handkerchief, so," and the old gentleman drew out a large silk handkerchief from the pocket that was next to Ruby. "Then she spreads it upon my shoulder just so,—and I put my arm about her, and she cuddles up to me and puts her head down on the handkerchief and takes a nice nap. Then when she wakes up we are almost ready to get off, and she has not minded the long ride. I wonder if you would not like to put your head down here a few minutes, and see if you like it as well as Ellie does. And then if such a thing should happen as that you should go to sleep, why, that would be so much the better."

Ruby hesitated. She did not feel as if any one who was old enough to go to boarding-school ought to be such a baby as to go asleep on the way, but she was very tired. She had awakened almost before it was light that morning, and she had been so excited over her journey that she could not keep still for a moment, and then the long ride was making her still more tired. The handkerchief, and the strong arm looked very inviting, and when she looked back and saw that Aunt Emma had gone to sleep, too, that quite decided her.

She slipped up nearer to the old gentleman, and taking off her hat, handed it to him to put up in the rack over head. Then she laid her head down upon the silk handkerchief, and he put his arm about her, and drew her up closely to him.

"It makes me think of the way papa holds me," she said, but the thought of her papa made two big tears splash down upon the silk handkerchief.

"Shall I tell you where I went with my father when I was a little boy," the old gentleman asked,—without seeming to notice the tears,—and then he began a long story which somehow put the tired little girl fast asleep, and the next thing she knew, Aunt Emma was telling her that it was time for her to think about getting her hat on, for they had almost reached their journey's end.

"Have I boon asleep?" asked Ruby, starting up and rubbing her eyes.

"I should say so," said the old gentleman, looking at his watch. "Guess how long a nap you have taken, little girl."

"Ten minutes?" asked Ruby, who thought she must only have just closed her eyes, since she could not remember having slept at all. The last thing that she remembered was listening to the old gentleman's story, and then it had seemed as if the very next thing was being awakened by Aunt Emma's voice.

"Ten minutes, and ever so much more," the old gentleman answered with a smile. "You have been asleep just two hours."

"Two hours!" and Ruby's eyes were wide open with surprise. "Why, I never remembered that."

"You were sleeping too sound to remember anything," her friend said.

"Well, I am glad you have had a nice rest, and now you will enjoy reaching your journey's end all the more. I shall miss you very much when you get out, for you have been very pleasant company."

"I wasn't very nice when I was asleep, I am afraid," said Ruby, "It was n't very polite of me to go to sleep, was it?"

"Oh, yes it was when I invited you to," the gentleman said. "And I enjoyed it, for it seemed just like having my little granddaughter here with me."

Aunt Emma helped Ruby put her hat on straight, and brushed the dust from her dress. The engine began to whistle, and that meant that they were very near a station.

Ruby said good-by to her kind friend, and he gave her his card with his name upon it, and asked her to write him a letter after she had been at school a little while and tell him how she liked it, and how she was getting on in her lessons.

Ruby promised that she would; and then the train began to go more slowly, and at last stopped with a little jerk at a station, and Aunt Emma said,—

"Here we are at last, Ruby."

For just a moment Ruby was not glad. She suddenly began to feel a little shy about boarding school, and remembered what she had not thought much about before,—that she would have to meet a great many strange girls, and that it would take some time to become acquainted with them,—and she wished again, as she had wished many times before, that Ruthy might have come with her; but she had not much time to think about anything, for the train did not wait very long for people to get out, and in a few moments Aunt Emma and Ruby were on the platform of the station and Ruby was waving good-by to the kind old gentleman, who was leaning out of the window to see the last of his little friend.

CHAPTER XI.

AN OLD ACQUAINTANCE.

There were several cars, and a great many people got out of them, for this was a junction, and some who were not going to stop here got out that they might take a train that would carry them where they wanted to go.

"We must wait till I see about our trunks," said Aunt Emma; and leaving Ruby in a safe corner, she went to look after the baggage and give the checks to the expressman who was waiting to take the trunks up to the school.

Ruby stood very still looking about her. It was a very busy place, and there was a good deal to see. After the train upon which she had come had drawn out of the station and gone puffing and panting upon its way, so that she could not see her friend the kind old gentleman any more, another train came into the station that was going the other way, and a few people got off, while a great many of those who were waiting in the station got upon it.

A lady with a little girl and a great many bags and bundles got off this last train, and perhaps you can guess how surprised Ruby was when she found it was some one whom she knew.

I wonder if you could guess who it was. I do not believe you could, so I will tell you. It was Maude Birkenbaum and her mother who had come upon this other train.

"Oh, I so wonder if she is going to boarding-school too," thought Ruby. "I never, never spected to see that girl again, but I don't know but what I am maybe a very little glad to see her, for I don't know one single other of the girls here, and it would be so lonesome for a while. She sha'n't make me do bad things now anyhow, for I am ever so much older than I was when she got me into so many troubles that summer."

Ruby had been told not to go away from the place where Aunt Emma had left her, so even to speak to Maude she would not leave it; but she did not need to, for in a few minutes Mrs. Birkenbaum went to the baggage-room, and Maude walked about looking around her.

In a little while her eyes fell upon Ruby, and she rushed forward with an exclamation of pleasure.

"Why, Ruby Harper!" she exclaimed, quite as much surprised at seeing Ruby as Ruby had been to see her. "I never thought of your being here. What are you doing here anyway?"

"I am going to boarding-school," answered Ruby, "and that is my trunk;" and she pointed to her pretty little black trunk, which the expressman was putting upon the wagon, that was getting quite a load of baggage by this time.

"I wonder if you are going to the same school that I am," said Maude. "I do hope you are, for then we can have such good times together. I am going to Miss Chalmer's Home Boarding-School for Young Ladies. Where are you going?"

"I don't know," admitted Ruby, unwillingly. It had never occurred to her to ask her Aunt Emma the name of the school; indeed I do not think that she knew that any school had a particular name any more than the school at home did. That was always called the school, and so Ruby had thought that this new school was simply a boarding-school. How dreadful it would be if Maude was going to a Boarding-School for Young Ladies, and she herself should be going to a school for children.

"You don't know," echoed Maude. "How funny. You are just as funny as ever, Ruby Harper. I never heard of any one starting out to go to boarding-school without knowing where they were going."

"Well, I did n't need to know, or I should have asked," said Ruby, with some dignity. "I came with my Aunt Emma, and she is a teacher in this school that I am going to, and so I did not have to know anything about it. She brought me with her."

"Oh," said Maude, in more respectful tones.

To have an aunt who taught in a boarding-school was a great thing in Maude's eyes, and it made her less inclined to patronize Ruby.

"I do hope it is the same school," she went on presently, really glad in the bottom of her selfish little heart to see some one whom she had known before, for this was her first time too of leaving home. "We will have such nice times together, and I have ever and ever so many things to show you. You just ought to see all the dresses I have brought with me."

"And so have I," Ruby answered. "My trunk is just full of them, and I had a dressmaker sewing them for a whole week before I came away from home."

"Did you?" asked Maude, and Ruby was pleased to notice that she spoke as if this fact made her have a higher opinion of Ruby. "I thought your mamma always made your dresses."

"She always used to, but she is sick now," said Ruby, and the lump rose in her throat again at the thought that she was miles away from her mother. "So we had Miss Abigail Hart come and stay a whole week and sew on them all the time."

"You must have a nice lot then," said Maude. "I am glad, for if we are going to be friends, I should not like to have the other girls think that you looked old-fashioned and as if you came from the country;" and foolish little Maude tossed her head, and looked complacently down upon her pretty travelling-dress.

Perhaps if Ruby had not been thinking about her mother just then, she would have been very angry at Maude's words, and the two children would have begun to quarrel at once; but thinking of her promise to her mother, the very last thing, that she would really try to be good, and do just what she knew was right, Ruby controlled the hasty words, and said pleasantly,—

"Well, even if my dresses are not as pretty as yours, Maude, the girls won't think that it is your fault. Here comes Aunt Emma. Won't she be surprised to find that I know somebody here in this strange place?"

Aunt Emma was quite as surprised as Ruby had supposed she would be, and presently Maude's mamma came up, and was very glad to find that Maude was going to have an old friend for a school-fellow.

"Ruby is a good little girl, and she will keep Maude straight, I hope," she said to Ruby's aunt; and it was all Ruby could do to keep from looking as proud as she felt, to think that Maude's mamma should say that she was a good little girl.

Ruby did not feel as if she quite deserved the praise, but it was very pleasant nevertheless. She made up her mind that she would really try to be good and keep from getting angry at Maude when she said provoking things, and if possible she would help Maude to be good instead of doing wrong things that she proposed.

By this time all the trunks were in the wagon and on their way to the school; and Ruby and Maude, with Aunt Emma and Mrs. Birkenbaum, set out to walk, for it was not a very great distance.

The two little girls walked together in front, and the ladies came after more slowly.

"I wonder what boarding-school will be like," said Ruby presently.

"I suppose it will be perfectly dreadful," said Maude. "I know some girls that went to boarding-school once, and they told me that it was awful. They never had enough to eat, and they had to study all the time, and they got so homesick that they tried to run away, but the teacher caught them and brought them back again."

Ruby looked horrified.

"Do you spose that was really true that they did not have enough to eat?" she asked.

"Of course it's true, for these girls told me so," Maude answered. "I have brought a whole lot of cake and candy in my trunk, and I will give you some when I eat it, Ruby. My mamma is going to send me a box every month, so they sha'n't starve me, anyway."

Ruby turned back and exclaimed,—

"Aunt Emma, do they give the girls enough to eat at this school?"

Aunt Emma laughed.

"Why, of course they do," she answered. "Whatever put that notion into your head, Ruby? The girls have all they can eat of good, wholesome food, and it is just as nice as it is at home."

Ruby looked contented, and went on again.

"I did n't spose you would go and ask your aunt about what I said," Maude remarked presently in rather annoyed tones. "Now don't tell her one single word about the cake and candy I have in my trunk, or she may tell the other teachers, and they will take it away from me. I know all about what things the teachers will do at boarding-school."

"I guess my auntie would n't do anything mean," Ruby answered rather hotly. "Anyway, Maude, perhaps this boarding-school is n't like the one that those girls went to. Aunt Emma said it would be ever so nice here, and she ought to know, for she has lived here ever since I was a little bit of a girl. I was only three years old when she began to teach here."

"Perhaps it is nice, and then perhaps again she has got used to it, and don't notice that it is n't pleasant," said Maude. "Anyway, I am ever so glad that you are here, Ruby, for it will be ever so much pleasanter having somebody I know."

"Turn the corner now, Ruby," called Aunt Emma, as the little girls came to the corner of a street, and going around the corner they found that they were close to the school.

Both the children were sure that it must be the school even before Aunt Emma said,—

"Here we are, girls. Does it not look like a pleasant place?"

It did, indeed, look very pleasant, and even Maude, who was disposed to find fault, could not raise any objection to the large, rambling brick house, with wide porches running all around it, shaded with vines, and surrounded on every side by large lawns and a pretty garden.

A row of great elms spread their wide branches upon both sides of the street, and just opposite the school stood a pretty church, with its spire reaching up among the trees, and ivy climbing over its stone walls.

Several little girls about as large as Ruby and Maude, as well as a few older ones, were amusing themselves upon the lawn, and they all looked very happy.

"Well, Maude, this is n't as bad as you thought it was going to be, is it?" asked Maude's mamma.

"No," admitted Maude. "It looks nice enough outside, but remember, mamma, if I don't like it I am going to run away and come home."

Aunt Emma looked at Maude, when she heard the little girl talking this way, and began to feel sorry that she had come, if she was going to say such naughty things. She did not want Ruby to have for a friend a little girl who would be more likely to help her get into mischief than to help her be good.

Maude looked up and saw Miss Emma's eyes fixed upon her with grave disapproval, and then she remembered that she had been talking about running away before one of the teachers.

"Oh, I don't really mean that," she said. "I won't run away, for papa said if I stayed and was good he would give me a watch that really goes and keeps time, for Christmas."

"I am glad you did not mean it," said Miss Emma. "You need not be afraid of being unhappy if you are good and obey the rules. Of course you will miss your mamma and papa for a little while, but you will soon be so interested in your studies and play that you will be contented, I hope. Our little girls are all very happy after the first few days."

Just then they entered the gate, and Ruby felt quite shy as she took hold of her aunt's hand, and stayed close beside her.

There were so many strange little girls that Ruby thought she would never get acquainted with all of them. She was not used to feeling shy, but then she had never seen so many strangers before. They went up the steps, upon the shaded porch,—where two little girls were sitting in a hammock reading, and looked as if they were birds in a nest,—-and rang the bell. Aunt Emma raised the great knocker upon the front door and rapped loudly.

Ruby was quite interested in looking at the knocker while they were waiting for the door to be opened. It was a lion's head, and it looked very fierce with its open mouth and sharp teeth. She wondered if she could reach it and rap with it if she stood on tiptoe, and she was just going to ask Aunt Emma to let her try, when the door opened, and a maid took them into the parlor.

Ruby looked about her with wondering eyes. So this was boarding-school.

CHAPTER XII.

MAKING ACQUAINTANCE.

They did not have to wait long for Miss Chapman, the principal of the school, to come in. Almost before the girl had closed the parlor door, and before Ruby had had time to do much more than glance about the room, the door opened again, and the dearest and sweetest of Quaker ladies came in. She had on a plain gray dress, and a white handkerchief was folded about her neck. She wore a little white cap over her silver hair, and her eyes were so kind that Ruby was quite sure that she should love her very, very much, and should never do anything to displease her if she could help it.

Miss Chapman greeted Aunt Emma very warmly, and was introduced to Mrs. Birkenbaum, and then she turned to the children.

"So these are the little girls I have been expecting," she said, shaking hands with them.

She asked them a few questions about their journey, and whether they had come together, and then she talked again with the ladies.

While this conversation was going on, the children looked about them, Maude no less curiously than Ruby, for boarding-school was a new experience to her, too.

It was a pleasant room. In one corner of it was a table with a globe upon it, and some books, and in another corner was a what-not, with shells and other curious things that Ruby wished she might go over and examine.

She was wondering whether she might not whisper to Aunt Emma how eager she was to go over to the what-not, and ask whether she might do so, when Miss Chapman rose, and took the party up to their rooms. Ruby was to room with her Aunt Emma, which was a very good arrangement for more than one reason; for she would be less apt to be homesick with her aunt, and besides that she would not be in danger of transgressing rules by speaking to other pupils after the lights had been put out for the night.

Maude was to room with one of the other girls, and her room was at the end of the hall. It was a very comfortable little room with two little white beds in it, but Maude did not seem very well satisfied with it. The room in which Ruby was to sleep was larger, because it was a teacher's room, and it did not please Maude to find that Ruby or indeed any one else, should have anything that was better than what she herself had. She looked very sullen, but she did not say anything while Miss Chapman was upstairs.

After Miss Emma and Ruby had gone to their own room and she was left alone with her mother in the room which she was to share, she threw herself down upon one of the beds, exclaiming angrily,—

"I don't want to stay here, mamma. I just wish you would either make them give me the nicest room in the house, or take me home with you. Do you spose I want a mean little room like this when Ruby Harper has such a nice one? The idea of a little country girl having a better room than I have! I won't stay if I have to have this room, so."

"Oh, yes," said Mrs. Birkenbaum, soothingly. "Yes, you will stay, Maude. The only reason that Ruby has a larger room is because it is her aunt's room, and of course a teacher has to have a larger and nicer room than the scholars. It will be ever so much nicer to be in this room. I am sure you would not like to be in the same room with a teacher and have her listening to everything you said. And now mind, you must be careful what you say to Ruby, for she will probably tell her aunt everything, and the teachers won't like you if you complain about things. Don't fuss about the room, that is a good child, and I will send you a new ring, and you shall have a great big box of cake every month, and then all the other girls will want to be friends with you. This is a nice room; see, it has two windows."

But Maude did not feel disposed to let herself be coaxed into liking the room.

"It's a horrid little bit of a room," she repeated again, pettishly. "I don't like it, and I won't stay, unless you send me a beautiful ring. What kind of a ring will it be, if I stay, mamma?"

"What kind of a ring would you like?" asked her mother. "You shall tell me just what you would like, and I will coax papa to buy it for you."

"I want a ring with red and blue stones in it," said Maude, sitting up, and looking less unhappy now that she was interested in her ring. "If papa will send me a ring like that then maybe I will stay, but you must remember to send me lots of cake and candy."

"Very well, dear, I will," said her mother, pleased at having coaxed the wilful little girl into submission.

"And you will be good, too, won't you, Maude? You know papa wants you to learn something, and you won't learn anything at home, so we want you to get along in your lessons here. Don't let little Ruby Harper beat you in everything. You are ever so much smarter than she is, if you only study."

"I guess I am smarter," said Maude, tossing her head. "Ruby is only a country girl, and I guess I can beat her in lessons and everything else if I make up my mind to it, but if I study you must give me everything I want for Christmas."

"Yes, we will," her mother answered. "Now get up and let me brush your hair, Maude, and we will go downstairs for a little while, and look about, and then I will unpack your trunk, and get things settled for you."

Maude felt better-natured by this time, so she got up from the bed, and let her mother brush her hair, and forgot to complain about things, or make bargains concerning her Christmas presents, while she looked through the window and watched the girls playing ring-toss down on the lawn.

"The girls that go to this school are n't one bit stylish," she said presently. "I guess I shall have nicer clothes than any of them. I wonder if they are nice girls. Do you spose I shall like them, mamma?"

"Oh, yes, I am sure you will," said her mother, encouragingly. "They are very nice, I am sure, and you will be so happy here that you won't hardly want to come home for the holidays. It won't be long before Christmas comes, so if you get homesick you must remember that."

"I guess I won't be homesick, if I can do as I want, and have plenty of candy and cake," said Maude, carelessly. "I am glad Ruby Harper is here, I shall not be so lonely then."

"You must give her some of the things I send you," said her mother.

"I will see," said Maude. "If she does as I want her to I will, but I am not going to give them all away. I want to keep some for myself."

"Now your hair looks all right," said her mother, giving one last brush to the waves of tightly crimped hair that fell below Maude's waist. "We will go downstairs and see the school-room, and look about the garden."

In the mean time Ruby had been helping Aunt Emma unpack her little trunk and she was so impatient to see what was in the mysterious package that Orpah had given her that she could scarcely wait for the trunk to be unlocked.

She lifted it out, and laid it on the bed, and untied the string.

"See if you can guess what is in it," she said to Aunt Emma.

"I guess a work-box," Aunt Emma said.

"I can't guess at all," Ruby answered, as she opened the paper, and found another wrapping of tissue paper covering the gift.

"Oh, Aunt Emma, what do you spose it is? See how carefully it is wrapped up."

She unfolded the tissue paper, and then she gave a little scream of delight. I think you would have been just as delighted as Ruby herself was, if you had had such a beautiful gift.

It was a little writing-desk, with a plate on the top, with the word Ruby engraved upon it, and a lock in front, with a little key in it. When Ruby turned the key, and opened the lid, she was more delighted even than she had been at first; for surely, no little girl ever had a prettier desk, with a more complete outfit in it.

There was a pretty little inkstand in one little compartment, with a silver top which screwed on so tightly that the ink could not possibly spill out when Ruby carried the desk around, and in the opposite compartment was a little silver box for stamps. There was a place for pen-holders and pencils, and when Ruby took off its cover and looked into it, she found the dearest pen-holder of silver, with her initial upon it, and a pen in it all ready for use. There was a little silver pencil in it too, that opened and shut, when it was screwed and unscrewed. Then there was a place for paper, and envelopes, and another place in which to keep all the dear home letters, that Ruby knew she was going to receive every week.

The envelopes were pink and cream, and chocolate and a pale blue, to match the paper, and they all had "H" upon them just as if they had been made especially for Ruby.

Orpah had directed one of the envelopes to herself, and put a stamp upon it all ready for Ruby to write to her.

All this was enough to make Ruby forget that she was tired and away from home, and to make her eyes shine like stars; but there was still something else, that I think she liked better than everything else in the desk put together.

Perhaps, it was because it was something that she had never dreamed that she should possess for her very own, that she was so delighted with it. There was a little outfit of sealing-wax, with sticks of different-colored wax, tiny tapers, and a little candlestick just big enough to hold such wee bits of candles, in the shape of a pond lily, and a little seal with "R" on it. So when Ruby had written her letters and put them in their envelopes, she could light one of the little tapers, drop some wax upon the back of the envelope, and press it down with the seal, just as she had seen her papa do.

"Oh, oh, oh," she cried, in delight. "I do think Orpah is just the nicest girl. Did you ever see anything quite so perfectly lovely, Aunt Emma? You shall use it when you write letters, if you want to, and oh, may I write a letter this very minute, and seal it with my seal?"

"Not just this minute, dear," said her aunt, smiling at her eagerness. "Wait until we have unpacked our trunks, and get a little settled, and then you may write and tell your mamma what a nice journey you had, and how kind the old gentleman was to you."

It was a very sure indication that Ruby was trying to be good, that she did not fret because she could not do as she wished that very minute. She put the things back in her desk, closed it, and locked it with the pretty little key, and said,

"Aunt Emma, I do wish I had a little ribbon so I could wear this key around my neck."

"I have a nice little piece of blue ribbon that I will give you as soon as I open my trunk," Aunt Emma said; and very soon Ruby had the cunning little key tied fast around her neck, where she could put up her hand and feel it every now and then, and think of the pretty gift, and above all of the sealing-wax, which was the chief charm of the desk.

CHAPTER XIII.

GETTING SETTLED.

Both Ruby and Maude felt very shy when they went downstairs and saw so many girls whom they did not know at all. They were very glad that among all those strange girls there was at least one whom they each knew.

"Was n't it the funniest thing that we should happen to come to the same boarding-school?" whispered Maude, as she took Ruby's hand and walked up and down the porch, while the scholars who had already come and felt very much at home, looked at them half curiously and half shyly, no doubt wondering whether they would be pleasant schoolmates or not.

Aunt Emma found that Ruby was quite contented to stay with Maude, so she went back upstairs, where she still had some little things to do, and Mrs. Birkenbaum finished unpacking Maude's things, for she had to go away that afternoon, and wanted to unpack Maude's trunk before she left.

Ruby and Maude walked up and down the porch for a time and then they went down upon the lawn. There was a large lawn in front of the house, where the girls usually played. In one corner of it there was a croquet set, and as this was something new to Ruby, she looked at the hoops with a great deal of interest, while Maude, who had a set at home explained the game to her.

"I will show you how to play it, and we will play together sometimes," Maude said.

There was plenty of room to play tag, and puss in the corner, and Ruby thought the trees grew in just the right places for that game. She wondered if there had been a school there when they were planted, and if Miss Chapman had planted them so that they would be nice for puss in the corner.

The house was quite large, and when Ruby and Maude walked around the lawn towards the back of the house, they found the schoolhouse, which was connected with the rest of the house by a long covered passage-way, so that the girls could go backward and forward in wet weather without getting wet.

The school-room was not open, but the children looked through the window, and saw the teacher's desk at one end, blackboards hung upon the walls, and long rows of desks and seats for the scholars.

On the other side of the school-room was the garden, with vegetables and flowers, and some pear-trees that were laden with fruit.

"Those pears look nice, don't they?" said Maude. "I wonder if they will let us have some. Perhaps Miss Chapman keeps them all for herself. We will have some anyway, won't we, Ruby. Well, I guess we have seen everything now. I think I will go upstairs and see if mamma has finished unpacking my trunk."

Ruby was quite willing to go into the house, for she was sure that by this time Aunt Emma would have emptied her trunk, and she might write her letter home.

"I was just coning to look for you, Ruby dear," said Aunt Emma, as her little niece opened the door. "You can write to your mamma now, if you like, and you will just have time to write a nice long letter before it is supper-time."

Ruby untied the ribbon about her neck, took the little key off, and opened the desk, with a feeling of pride. She was quite sure that there could not be a prettier desk in all the world than this one which Orpah had given her, and she was very anxious to show it to Maude, and surprise her with its beauty.

"What shall I write my letter on first, Aunt Emma?" she asked.

"Here is a piece of paper and a pencil you can use, and then you can copy it afterwards," said Aunt Emma; so Ruby sat down at a little table by the window, and wrote to her mother.

RUBY WRITING A LETTER HOME.

When she had finished her letter and Aunt Emma had looked it over, and corrected the few mistakes in spelling that she found, Ruby opened the desk, and putting it upon the table, took out some of her pink paper, which she thought was the prettiest, and carefully copied the letter.

"This ought to be a very nice letter, written on such a beautiful desk, with a silver pen-holder, ought n't it, Aunt Emma?" she asked.

"Yes, dear, and I am sure your mamma will think it is very nice," her aunt answered.

Ruby was very proud when she finished copying it without one single mistake. She did not usually have the patience to work so carefully but she felt as if such a desk deserved great care on the part of its owner.

Would you like to hear her letter? Here it is:

MY DEAR MAMMA AND PAPA,—I am writing this letter to you on a beautiful new desk that Orpah gave me. That was what was in the package she made me promise not to open. We had a very pleasant journey. There was a very kind old gentleman on the cars, who talked to me and told me stories, and he told the boy with a basket to let the little lady choose what she wanted, and I chose a big pear. I divided it with Aunt Emma and the old gentleman. When I was sleepy I put my head down on his shoulder the way his little grand-daughter does, and I went to sleep and I slept ever so long, though I thought it was only a little while. It is nice to ride in the cars, but it takes a long time. I like this school. I like Miss Chapman. She has white hair like grandma. Her eyes are blue. I shall be good, for I like her very much. But I shall be good anyway, because I promised you. I do want to see you, mamma, and papa, too. Aunt Emma has unpacked my trunk, and my things are all put away. Maude Birkenbaum is here. She was at the station at the same time I was, and we walked up together. I mean to be good. Her mother said she hoped I would be a help to Maude, and I mean to try to be good, instead of doing things she wants me to do. I love you a whole heartful, mamma and papa. Please write me a long letter soon. I hope you will soon be well again, mamma. I shall seal this letter with my new sealing wax, and you must pretend it is a kiss.

Your loving   RUBY.

Ruby was so impatient to use her new sealing-wax outfit that she found it very hard work to finish her letter carefully, and write the last words just as well as she had written the first one.

"Do you think 'Ruby' looks as well as 'My dear Mamma and Papa'?" she asked Aunt Emma, carrying the paper over to her.

That was Ruby's test whether she had been careful in writing a letter, to look and see whether the last words were as carefully written as the first ones. Sometimes, if she had not been very careful, one would not think that the same little girl had written all the letter. The first few lines would be so very neat and carefully written, and the last ones would be straggly, and of different heights and wandering all across the pages.

But this time Ruby had been very careful indeed. She had left just the same margin all the way down the left-hand side of her page, and she had been careful in dividing her words, so when Aunt Emma had looked it all over very carefully, she could say that it was just as nice as Ruby could possibly have written.

Then Ruby folded it and put it into one of her new envelopes; and then came the most exciting part of all. Ruby had never been very fond of letter-writing before, but she thought she would be perfectly willing to write a letter every day, if she might always seal them up with wax.

She put the little pond-lily candlestick out upon the table, on a folded piece of paper, which Aunt Emma told her she had better put under it lest the melted wax should drop upon the table-cloth, and then she took out her little box of colored tapers, and tried to decide which one she should use first.

She decided upon the pink one, because that matched the color of the paper she had been using; and so she took out a pink taper, and set it in the candlestick. It fitted very snugly, so there was no danger of its falling out.

Aunt Emma showed her how to open the little silver match-box that Ruby had not discovered before in the outfit, and she lighted the taper, and then held a stick of green sealing-wax in the flame.

When the end had grown quite soft in the heat, Ruby watched it carefully, and let the big drop at the end fall just at the right time, and in just the right place upon her envelope. Then she pressed the seal down upon it, and you can guess how proud she was when she saw her initial in the wax.

"Won't mamma be surprised when she gets this letter?" she asked gleefully. "She will wonder where I got the wax, and I am sure she will hardly believe that I made such a nice seal the very first time I ever used it."

her, which made a very great difference; and then she was very much interested in listening to the talk of the girls who had been there before, as they crowded about Aunt Emma and told her of what they had been doing during their vacation.

Maude was not at all pleased when she found that no one paid any particular attention to her, and she sat by herself with a very discontented look upon her face.

One of the girls came up to her after a time, and asked her if she would like to take part in a game, but Maude refused, sullenly, and after that no one else spoke to her.

"I shall go home just as soon as mamma can come and get me," she said to herself. "I don't like this place one single bit. No one pays a bit of attention to me, and my dress is ever so much nicer than any one else's. I think Ruby might come and sit by me, instead of staying with her aunt, so I do."

But Ruby was very happy where she was. She had not forgotten Maude, and when they had first gone into the sitting-room, she had invited Maude to come and sit beside her; but as Maude had refused, wishing Ruby to come over to her, she had concluded that Maude wished to be by herself, and was listening to the talk going on about her, without thinking any more about Maude.

At eight o'clock all the girls went up to bed, and Miss Chapman told them that in half an hour a bell would be rung, and that then they must put their lights out, and not talk any more to one another that night.

Some of the girls who were tired had gone to bed earlier, but most of the scholars had stayed downstairs until that hour. The next day would be the first day of regular school, and Miss Chapman told them that she hoped they would all sleep well so as to be fresh for their studies in the morning.

When Ruby was in her room, she realized for the first time with all her heart how much happier she was than those girls who had come quite alone. If she had not Aunt Emma she did not know what she should have done, she should have been so lonely. As it was, all her chatter stopped as she began to get undressed, and though Aunt Emma talked on about everything that she thought would interest her little niece, yet Ruby's answers grew more and more infrequent, and Aunt Emma guessed that she was thinking about home, and the dear ones there from whom she had never been separated so long before.

Ruby was really a brave little girl, and when she felt the lump swelling in her throat again she kept swallowing it back, and trying to think only of how pleased her papa would be when he should hear that she had been good and had not cried to come home; but when at last she knelt down to say her prayers in her little white night gown, the tears would come.

"I want mamma, oh, I want mamma," she sobbed.

Aunt Emma took her up tenderly in her arms, and kissed and comforted the little girl as tenderly as she could; but no one could take the place of mother, and though Ruby tried to stop crying, the tears came fast and thick.

"You may think I am not trying to be brave, Aunt Emma," said Ruby, through her sobs; "but I am trying, I truly am, but it does just seem as if I should die if I could n't see my mamma. Oh, if I was only home again. Can't I possibly go home to-morrow, Aunt Emma? Do say yes, or I can't live all night."

"There, dear, don't cry so hard," said Aunt Emma, wiping away her tears. "You will feel better to-morrow, Ruby darling. You will be so busy getting your lessons that you will not have time to think about anything else, and then when night comes again, you will remember that you have come away with me so that your dear mamma can get well and strong again, and the braver you are, the sooner she will improve. You had forgotten that, had n't you, dear? You know you are helping to make her well here at school. I know you can't help crying some. I shall not think you are not brave because you do, but I know you are going to stop very soon and cuddle up and go to sleep, and wake up as happy as a little bird."

Ruby wiped away her tears after a time, and Aunt Emma went to bed with her, that the little girl might feel loving arms about her, and not remember how far she was away from home and from her mother and father.

CHAPTER XIV.

SCHOOL.

At half-past six the next morning, the rising-bell sounded through the house, and Ruby sat up in bed and rubbed her eyes, trying to remember where she was, and what the bell was.

It did not take her very long to remember, and she jumped out of bed quite happy again, and wondering what the first day of school would be like.

By the time she was all dressed, and had put on one of her pretty new school dresses, the bell rang again, and as Ruby followed Aunt Emma out into the hall, she saw that all the other doors down the long passage-way were opening, and the girls were coming out, some of them fastening their collars, as if they had not had quite time enough to dress.

They went down to the dining-room and sat in their chairs around the sides of the room while Miss Chapman read morning prayers. Miss Chapman was seated in her large chair at the end of the room when the girls entered, looking, as Ruby thought to herself, like a queen upon her throne. As they came in one after another, each one said, "Good morning, Miss Chapman," and she answered them.

Some of the girls, those who had been there the year before, made a little courtesy as they entered, but the new scholars were too shy to even try to do this, and they only said "Good morning," and some of them were so shy that their lips only moved, and not even the girl next to them could hear what they were trying to say.

After prayers came breakfast, and then the girls went upstairs to make their beds and put their rooms in order. There were sixteen girls altogether, and two teachers besides Miss Chapman and Miss Emma, as the girls called her. There was Miss Ketchum, and Mrs. Boardman, who was really the matron, though the girls always thought of her as a teacher, and she sometimes taught a class if any of the other teachers were ill or away.

Mrs. Boardman went around to the rooms and told the girls how the rooms were to be kept, and she was such a motherly, warm-hearted body that very often if she found a homesick girl in her room she would know just how to cheer and comfort her, and help her to dry her tears.

Poor little Maude was really very unhappy. Her room-mate had not come yet, so she was all alone in her room, and when Mrs. Boardman went in she found her packing her trunk again, with her tears falling fast and thick upon her dresses. For once she did not care whether they were spoiled or not. All she thought of was to go home again as fast as she could, and it had not entered her head that she might not be permitted if she really made up her mind to go.

Before Mrs. Birkenbaum had gone, she had told Miss Chapman that Maude would probably want to come home, and that they would have hard work keeping her, as she was used to having her own way, so Mrs. Boardman was not very much surprised when she saw what Maude was doing.

Maude did not look up when the teacher entered the room. She was very homesick, poor child, and then besides her desire to see her father and mother, she was very much aggrieved because no one had paid any special attention to her. She had been used to having people make a great deal of her because her clothes were so fine, and here no one had seemed to notice nor care whether she was better dressed than the others or not.

This was a new experience to the little girl, and she did not like it. Even Ruby had been more noticed than she had been, and she had always looked down upon Ruby because she lived in the country, and did not have fashionable clothes. It was quite too hard to bear, and Maude determined to go home.

"Wait a minute, my dear," said Mrs. Boardman, pleasantly. "That is n't what you ought to be doing just now. This is the time to make beds, and as your room-mate has not come, I will help you this morning, so you will not have to make it all alone; but perhaps you know how to make a bed, so that you would just as soon make it by yourself."

Maude lifted her face, her eye flashing through her tears.

"I don't know how to make a bed," she answered. "I never made a bed. My mamma has a servant make them at home, and she never had me do such a thing. I don't want to know how to make it, nor to do anything else. I want to go home. I am packing my trunk."

"But you can't go home, you know, my dear," said Mrs. Boardman, pleasantly. "I know just how you feel. When I was a little girl about your age I went away from home for a few weeks, and I am afraid I was n't very brave about it."

"Did you go to school?" asked Maude.

"No, but I will tell you where I went while we are making the bed. Now you take that side of the sheet, that is the way, and draw it up so, and tuck it in snugly, so your toes won't peep out in the night. Well, I was going to tell you how I happened to go away from home. One day when I came home from school, my father met me down by the gate and he told me that my little brother had the scarlet fever and the doctor thought that perhaps I might not have it, too, if they sent me right away, so I was to go to board with an old lady about ten miles away who was willing to take care of me. He had the carriage all ready,—now the blanket, dear; that's right,—and a bundle with the dresses in that I should want for a few weeks, and before I knew it I was on my way. I could n't even say good-by to my mother, for she was with my brother."

"And were you homesick?" asked Maude.

"Yes, indeed," answered Mrs. Boardman. "I cried and cried the first night, and I thought I would surely walk home the very first thing in the morning. I did not care whether I had the scarlet fever or not, if I might only go home; but when morning came I remembered what my father had said, when he bade me good-by, and so I changed my mind, and stayed."

"What had he said?" asked Maude, helping to turn the top of the sheet over, and quite forgetting, in her interest in the story, that she had not intended to make the bed.

"He had said when he kissed me good-by, 'Now I know that you will be very homesick, Eliza, and will want to come home a good many times, but I know that you are mother's brave, helpful little maid, and that I can trust you to stay here until brother gets well so that she will not worry about you.' Of course I was not going to disappoint my father when he trusted me; so though I was homesick enough and very unhappy, I stayed there for several weeks until the doctor said it was safe for me to go home again. But you see I remember just how it feels to be homesick, and feel as if one could n't stay away one single day more from home. It takes a brave girl to make up her mind that she will not give up to homesickness, but will do what she knows is going to please those whom she loves. Yes, I know that sounds as if I meant that I was brave, when I was a little girl, but then I really think I was, don't you?"

"Yes," admitted Maude. "I think I should have gone home if I had been in your place, and had only ten miles to walk. Did you have a nice time staying with the old lady?"

"No, it was not very pleasant," said Mrs. Boardman. "Now pat the pillow, this way, Maude, before you put it in its place, so. I did not have any lessons nor any books to read, and I had no time to bring my patchwork or knitting, and so the time hung very heavy on my hands. I helped about the work when there was anything that a little girl could do. I fed the hens, and looked for eggs, and wiped dishes, and sewed carpet rags, and sometimes I went with the hired man to bring the cows home. There, the bed looks very nicely now, does n't it? I think you will be able to make it look as well as that every day, don't you? And then when you go home again even if the servant does make it, you will not have to think that she knows how to do something which you do not know how to do. It is very nice to know how to do every useful thing, even if it may not be necessary to practise it. Suppose your mamma did not know how to make a bed, and she should have a servant who could not, how do you suppose she would show her without knowing herself? Now shall we hang up these dresses? It is almost time for the bell to ring, so I think you can put these away just as nicely as you could if I stayed and helped you, and then I can go and look after some of the other girls. Now I am going to say to you what my father said to me, 'You are a brave little maid,' and I know you are to be trusted to do what is right. I know you are going to forget all about how much you want to go home, and you are going to do the very best you know how to-day, so that your papa and mamma will be pleased with you;" and Mrs. Boardman hurried away, giving Maude a motherly little squeeze as she passed her.

Maude stood looking at her trunk for a few moments after Mrs. Boardman had gone away, rather undecided what to do with her dresses. Fifteen minutes before she had quite made up her mind that she was going home and that nobody in all the world should make her stay at boarding-school now that she had made up her mind that she did not like it, but Mrs. Boardman had taken it for granted that she was a good, brave little girl who wanted to do just what was right, and somehow Maude did not want to disappoint her.

Usually Maude's one aim in life was to do just what she chose, and to have her own way in

CHAPTER XV.

BEGINNING SCHOOL.

The school-room was very cheerful and pleasant. There were windows on both sides of the room, and all the space between the windows was covered with blackboards or maps.

Ruby began to feel really happy when she sat down on a bench with the new scholars, waiting to be examined by Miss Chapman and assigned to a class. She loved study, and was always happy during school-hours, and generally very good, too, for she was too busy to get into mischief, and too anxious to have a good report to wilfully break any rules. "I wonder if you are as far advanced as I am," whispered Maude, as she sat down beside Ruby.

It was on the tip of Ruby's tongue to tell her that she had been at the head of her class for a long time at home, but she remembered in time to check herself that it was not at all probable that whispering was allowed here more than in any other school, and that she might break a rule the very first thing if she should answer.

One by one Miss Chapman called the girls up to the desk where she sat, and questioned them about their studies and the books they had used, and Miss Ketchum, at her side, wrote down the answers in a little book. Then the girls were assigned a seat, and Miss Ketchum took their books to them, and showed them what the lesson would be.

Ruby was very much pleased when she found that she was to be in the class with girls who were, most of them, larger than herself, and as she was not at all shy, she could answer all the questions Miss Chapman asked her, very fluently, so that the teacher had a very good idea of what the little girl really knew.

Some of the new scholars were so shy that they could scarcely answer, and Miss Chapman knew that it would take two or three days to find out how far advanced they were.

Very much to Maude's surprise, she was put in a class below Ruby. She was not at all pleased with this, for it was a great mortification to her pride to find that the little country girl whom she had looked down upon was beyond her in her studies.

Maude had never attended school regularly, but had stayed at home whenever she could beg consent from her mother, and very often she had won it by teasing when there was really no reason at all why she should not have been at her desk. Even when she had attended school it had never occurred to her that it was for her own benefit that her teachers tried to have her learn her lessons. She had shirked them as much as possible, and as no teacher has time to waste over a little girl who will not study when there are so many willing to learn, she had managed to get along with very little study, and so, of course, had learned but little.

She was ashamed to see what small girls were in the class with her, and she made up her mind that she would study so hard that she would soon be promoted into the class in which Ruby had been put.

It took until recess time to arrange all the classes, and then the bell rang, and the scholars were free to go out upon the lawn for a half-hour. A basket of rosy-cheeked apples was passed about, and all the children were very ready for one. Some day-scholars attended this school, and Ruby thought, rather wistfully, how nice it would be if she, too, were going home when school should be out.

Maude did not care about being with Ruby during recess time, for she was afraid that Ruby would remember her speech early that morning, and remind her that she instead of Maude was the farthest advanced in her studies. Ruby was becoming acquainted with some of her new classmates, and was finding this first morning of school life very pleasant.

The rest of the morning seemed longer than the first part had done, and Ruby as well as most of the others were very glad when the noon intermission came. The day-scholars took out their lunch-baskets, and prepared to eat their lunches, and the bell rang for the boarding-scholars to go up to their rooms and get ready for dinner.

As each little girl reached the door, she stopped, turned around and made a courtesy to Miss Chapman who was sitting opposite the door. Ruby watched the girls as they went out one by one. She was quite sure that she could never make a courtesy, and as each girl passed out, her turn to go came nearer and nearer.

What should she do? If her Aunt Emma had only been there, Ruby might have asked her to let her stay in the school-room, for she felt as if she would a great deal rather go without her dinner than try to make a courtesy when she did n't know how, with all those girls looking at her. What if she should tumble down in trying to make it? It seemed very likely that she would, the very first time she had ever tried to do such a thing. The very thought of such an accident made Ruby's face grow redder than ever. Only three more girls and then Miss Chapman's eyes would be fixed upon her, and it would be time for her to get up and go out. Now only two more girls, and then the last one had gone, and Ruby knew that she must go.

She walked over to the door, feeling as shy as Ruthy had ever felt, and stood there a moment. How could she ever try to courtesy with all those girls looking at her?

She hesitated so long that all the girls looked up to see why she did not go out.

Ruby stood in the door one moment longer, and then she turned and ran down the passage-way as fast as she could go, feeling as if now she must surely go home, for she had disgraced herself forever.

She had come out of the room without courtesying, or even saying good-morning as all the other girls had done, and then her running away had of course made all the girls laugh at her.

What would Miss Chapman do to her? Would she give her bad marks, or put her at the foot of her class, or keep her in after school? Anything would be bad enough, but the worst of all to proud little Ruby was the thought that she had failed in doing something which all the other scholars seemed to have done so easily.

She sobbed aloud as she ran down the passage-way with her hands clasped tightly over her face, and as she turned the corner to go into the house, she ran straight into somebody's arms.

She uncovered her face and looked up as a familiar voice said, "Why, Ruby, where are you going so fast? I was just coming to look for you. But are you crying? Why, what is the matter?"

But Ruby was crying so hard that Aunt Emma could not understand what she said. She could only make out that it was something about courtesying, so she led Ruby up to her room, and quieted her down a little, and would not let her talk about her trouble until her hair was brushed and her face washed.

"I might have taught you how to courtesy before school-time this morning if I had only thought of it in time," Aunt Emma said. "But now you must n't cry about it any more, Ruby. Of course it would have been better if you had tried to do as the other girls did, but now all you can do is to tell Miss Chapman that you are sorry and that you will not do so any more, and you must not fret any more about it. I will show you now, and then you will courtesy as nicely as any one else, before you have to do it again."

"But, Aunt Emma, what made the girls do it?" asked Ruby. "If the first girl had not done it none of the others would have had to, would they? And I don't think it is one bit nice, and I don't see what they want to do it for. And oh, Aunt Emma, you ought to have seen how beautifully Maude courtesied. She did it the very best of all the girls, and I don't see how she knew about it, for I am sure she never did it before."

"I will tell you why the girls do it," Aunt Emma answered. "It is one of the rules of the school that when a scholar goes out of a room where there is a teacher, she must courtesy to the teacher as she leaves the room. That is intended as a mark of respect. Yesterday school had not begun, and so no attention was paid to it, but to-day everything is going on as usual as nearly as possible. It happened to be one of the old scholars who went out of the room first to-day, and so she knew about it. If it had been a new scholar Miss Chapman would have spoken to her about it. But remember, Ruby, even in the afternoon, if you are in the sitting-room with a teacher, to courtesy when you leave the room. It will not be at all hard after I show you how, and I would not like you to forget it."

"Oh, dear," groaned Ruby. "I never heard of anything so funny. Must I go and courtesy to you every time I go out of this room, Aunt Emma? Why, it will take all my time courtesying."

Aunt Emma laughed.

"Well, I think you may be excused from that when we are alone in the room together," she answered. "If I am in charge of the girls downstairs or in the school-room, then you must of course do just as you would if any other teacher was there, but up here I will excuse you, as I suppose it would seem like a good deal to you to remember a courtesy every time you went in or out of the room. Now I will show you. Look here;" and Aunt Emma courtesied.

Ruby was very much pleased to find that it was very easy to draw one foot behind the other and make a courtesy, and she was quite proud of her new accomplishment when she had practised it a few times.

"And now, Ruby dear," said Aunt Emma, looking at her watch, "there is just time before dinner for you to go and tell Miss Chapman you are sorry that you left the school-room in that way. She will not scold you, I am sure, so you need not be afraid to go and speak to her. She is in her own room at the end of the hall, and you had better go at once so as to have time before the bell rings."

"And then I will make a beautiful courtesy when I come out of her room, shall I?" asked Ruby, quite ready to go, since she would have a chance to show how nicely she could courtesy now.

Aunt Emma smiled.

"Yes," she answered.

Tap, tap, tap, went Ruby at Miss Chapman's door, and when she heard the teacher call, "Come in," she opened the door and walked in quite bravely.

Miss Chapman was sitting in her large chair by the window looking over some books.

She held out her hand to Ruby.

"Well, my dear," she said kindly.

"Please ma'am, I came to tell you that I am very sorry I ran out of school without courtesying," said Ruby, rather shyly, looking at the beautiful white hair while she was speaking, and wondering if when she herself grew to be an old lady she would ever have such beautiful fluffy hair, and if she should wear a little white cap.

"Why did you do so, Ruby?" asked Miss Chapman.

Ruby hung her head.

"I did not know how to courtesy," she answered presently. "And I was afraid I should fall down if I tried, it looked so hard, and I was afraid the girls would laugh at me if I tried and tumbled over; and it was so dreadful to have them all looking at me, and then know that I could n't do it, that I just could n't help running. But I know how now. Aunt Emma taught me, and I won't ever forget it now. Please excuse me for this morning."

"Yes," Miss Chapman answered. "I can quite understand how it happened this morning, and I am glad you will never do so again. I hope you are going to be a good little girl, Ruby, and progress nicely in your studies. You have had a good teacher and have been well taught, and know how to apply yourself, so I shall hope that you will stand well in your classes."

Ruby hardly knew what to say, so she blushed with pleasure, and did not answer.

"Now you can go," said Miss Chapman, and so Ruby walked over to the door, opened it, and turned around and stood exactly in the middle of the doorway. Then drawing back her foot, she made a very careful and deep courtesy, and gravely closed the door after her and ran back to Aunt Emma.

"Aunt Emma, there is something I have been thinking about," she said after she had told her aunt how kindly Miss Chapman had spoken to her. "This morning I almost got real mad at Maude, for she asked me in such a superior sort of way if I sposed we should be in the same class. 'Do you spose you are as far advanced as I am, Ruby?' she said, just as if she thought I was ever so much behind her. I was going to tell her I guessed I was just as smart as she was, but then I remembered it was school and I did n't, for I knew I must n't talk, but you would 't believe with what little girls she is. I am way ahead of her. Well, I did think I would just remind her of what she said, but I guess maybe I had n't better; for she certainly could courtesy when I didn't know the first thing about it, and so that sort of makes us even. She did n't see me run away, but then if she heard some one else say something about it, she would know, and I should n't feel very nice if she should tell me that anyway she knew something that I could n't do without being showed how. Don't you think I had n't better say anything about being ahead of her?"

"I am sure you had better not," said Aunt Emma, promptly; "but it is not because of the courtesying, Ruby, it is because it is not a kind thing to boast, or to remind any one else of their failings. You know you would not like it yourself, and that ought to be reason enough for your never doing it to any one else. What is the Golden Rule?"

"Do unto others as you would they should do unto you," repeated Ruby, promptly.

"Yes; and that means that you should never, never do to any one else anything that you would not like to have done to yourself," Aunt Emma said.

Just then the dinner-bell rang.

"I know what I will do," exclaimed Ruby, cheerfully. "I will go to Maude's room and go down to dinner with her, for I just spect she feels sort of lonesome. I saw her once at recess, and she was all by herself, and had n't any one to play with. I will stay with her till she gets a little more acquainted, and that will be paying attention to the Golden Rule; for if I was all by myself here, and had n't got you, Aunt Emma, I am sure I would be glad if Maude would stay with me;" and Ruby ran off to find her little friend, feeling as happy as if she had not had such a burst of tears but half an hour ago.

CHAPTER XVI.

MAUDE'S TROUBLES.

Poor little Maude had not been enjoying this first day at school. It had begun with tears, and she had just been having another burst of anger, and had thought that she could not possibly stay in such a school another hour. It was a new experience to the self-willed child to have to give up her own way, and submit to regulations that she did not like; and although she had managed the courtesy that had brought Ruby to grief, without the least trouble, as she had been to dancing-school, and could courtesy in the most approved French style, yet she found a great grievance waiting for her as soon as she reached her room.

Mrs. Boardman was waiting for her.

"Maude, I want to help you arrange your hair a little differently," she said. "Miss Chapman does not like the girls to wear their hair here at school as you wear yours, flying all over your shoulders. She does not think it neat, nor does she like little girls to pay so much attention to their appearance while they are at school. Of course she wants you to be neat, but not dressed up as if you were going to a party. She likes her scholars to wear their hair braided, and I will help you braid yours now, as I suppose you cannot do it alone if you are not used to it, and you have no room-mate yet to help you."

Maude looked at Mrs. Boardman in angry amazement.

If there was any one thing of which vain little Maude was prouder than another, it was of the crinkled, waving hair that fell below her shoulders. She rarely forgot it, and was always playing with a lock of it, or tipping her head over her shoulder, like a little peacock admiring his fine tail.

"I don't want to wear it braided," she exclaimed. "I like it this way. It would look like ugly little pig-tails if it was braided, and I won't have it that way. Oh, I want to go home. I don't like it here one single bit. I am sure my mamma would n't let me have my hair braided, like a little charity girl."

Mrs. Boardman was very patient with the spoiled child.

"Hush, dear; I would n't talk that way," she said. "I hoped your mamma had spoken to you about it before she went away, for I told her that Miss Chapman would want you to wear your hair differently. She told me that she wanted you to follow all the rules of the school, whatever they were; so I know she wishes you to wear your hair as Miss Chapman requires the others to wear their hair. Now, let me braid it for you, for it is growing near dinner-time."

But Maude threw herself down the bed, and began to cry.

"And now I must tell you about another rule," said Mrs. Boardman. "I expect it will seem to you as if we had a great many rules here; but you will soon get used to them, and then you will not find them burdensome. It is against the rules to sit upon your bed during the day-time. You see it will make the bed look untidy, and that is the reason for this rule. Now, we will straighten the bed out nicely, and then it will be quite tidy again."

Maude did not move.

"Oh, I must go home," she sobbed. "I can't stay here. It is a perfectly dreadful place. I have to do everything I don't like to do and I can't do the least little tiny thing that I like to do, and my beautiful hair will look so ugly, and I just can't stand it."

Some of the other teachers might have reproved the little girl for her fretful words, but kind-hearted Mrs. Boardman was too sorry for her. She could imagine how hard it must seem to a child who had never been under any control at all, to find herself obliged to obey rules, whether she liked them or not. She leaned over and stroked the golden hair.

"Now, dear, I know what a good little girl you are going to be when you think about it. I was very proud of you this morning, and thought I should like to have you for one of my special little friends very much. You see I am not exactly one of the teachers, and so I can have a pet when I want one. I know you don't like this rule, but then you are going to obey it because it is right and it will please your mother to know you are being a good girl. Something worse than having my hair braided happened to me when I was about your age. Jump up and let me braid your hair, and I will tell you about it. Come, dear. It is ever so much easier to do things because one wants to, you know, than because one is made to do them, and you will have to obey the rules whether you want to or not; so if I were in your place I should prefer to obey them of my own free will, because I wanted to do just what was right, and please my mother. I don't think you could guess what I had to have done to my hair."

Maude stood up and helped to pat the bed straight and flat again. She knew that, as Mrs. Boardman had said, she would have to obey the rules, whether she wanted to or not, and she did realize that it would be much more sensible to follow them willingly than to be in disgrace and be forced into compliance. And there was a better feeling than that in her heart, too.

She felt that she was in a place where no one cared for her clothes nor for the little airs she liked to put on, whenever she found any one to admire her, but where she would be valued just for herself, and for her behavior. In that one morning she had noticed how little girls who had not thought of themselves, but only of pleasing others, had found friends at once, while no one had seemed to care for her society; and she realized that if she was to have any love she must try to deserve it.

Mrs. Boardman was the one person who seemed willing to be her friend, and who tried to help her do right, and was patient with her ill-temper; and selfish little Maude was grateful for the first time in her life for kindness, and she did not want to disappoint any one who thought that she meant to be good.

She would try to be good, at any rate, even if it was not very pleasant.

After the bed was in order again, she stood still while Mrs. Boardman brushed her hair out and braided it for her.

"I must tell you what happened to my hair," she began cheerfully. "I had had typhoid fever, and my hair was all dropping out, so that the doctor said it must be shaved off. I did not want to have it shaved one bit, for it was quite long and had been thick, but of course I had to do as my mother said, and have it shaved. Oh, I felt so badly about it. I cried and cried the day it was all shaved off, and when I first looked at myself in the glass afterwards, I was almost frightened, I looked so dreadfully. Did you ever see any one's head after the hair had been shaved off?"

"No, ma'am," answered Maude.

"Well, then, you cannot imagine what it looks like. My head looked more like a ball than anything else, and where the hair had been it was perfectly smooth and bald, and there was only a purplish look to show where it had grown. I ran away and hid myself in the barn and cried harder than ever. But I had something nice happen to make up for all this."

"What was it?" asked Maude.

"When my hair grew again it was curly, and curly hair was what I had always wished for, and never expected to have; so you can imagine how delighted I was. There, see how nicely your hair looks now that I have braided it. Have you a ribbon to tie the ends?"

By the time Maude had found a ribbon and Mrs. Boardman had tied it at the ends of the braids, it was time for her to hurry away and look after some of the other girls; but Maude's face wore a very different expression from the tearful, angry one that had been upon it when she first heard that her hair must be braided. There was a wistful look in her eyes that made Mrs. Boardman turn back and give her a kiss. "We are going to be good friends, are we not, Maude?" she said. "And you are going to be so good that I shall be very proud to say, 'Maude is one of my special friends.'"

"Yes, ma'am, I will try to be good," Maude answered. "Thank you," she added, with unusual gratitude.

She was looking quite cheerful when Ruby came in.

"I was afraid you were lonesome, Maude," she exclaimed, "and I came to go down to dinner with you. When is your room-mate coming, do you suppose?"

"I don't know," Maude answered. "Mrs. Boardman said she thought she would come to-night, or maybe to-morrow morning."

"Are you glad you are going to have some one in the room with you?" asked Ruby.

"I don't know," Maude answered. "If she is nice, I will be glad, and if she is n't nice, I spose I shall be sorry. How did you like school this morning?"

"Ever so much," Ruby answered, enthusiastically. "Did n't you?"

"Not very much," Maude replied. "I think the lessons are awfully hard."

Ruby was very much tempted to say something that would have sounded rather boastful, but she checked herself.

It had been on the tip of her tongue to exclaim,—

"Why, if you think your lessons are hard, in a class like yours, what do you suppose mine must be, when I am in with such big girls;" but she only said,—

"I spose the first day everything seems harder; but when we get used to the teachers and the lessons, they won't seem so hard."

The dinner-bell rang, and Ruby exclaimed,—

"Oh, I am so hungry. It just seems as if I had not had anything to eat for a year. Let's hurry and go down before the rest, Maude."

But everybody else was hungry, too, so Ruby and Maude were by no means the first of the stream of girls that hurried into the dining-room.

CHAPTER XVII.

LEARNING.

I suppose you can hardly fancy a school where little girls were not allowed to wear their hair as they liked; where they had to courtesy to teachers when they left the room; and, what was still more surprising, had to eat whatever was given to them at the table. I think that such a school would seem so very old-fashioned nowadays that no little girls could be found who would be willing to go to it, and even in those days there were very few like it.

The dear old Quaker lady, Miss Chapman, taught the little girls to do just as she herself had been taught to do when she were a little girl; so you can easily imagine that her ways was not quite the ways of other teachers. And yet, since her scholars were as healthy, happy, rosy-cheeked little girls as you could find anywhere, I do not know that any one could complain that her ways were not very good ways. They seemed very strange to new scholars sometimes, if they had attended other schools where the rules were not so strict; but they very soon grew used to them, and then they did not mind them at all, and were very happy.

If Maude had not been sitting by her friend, Mrs. Boardman, perhaps she would have made a great fuss at dinner-time about eating the piece of sweet potato which had been served to her.

She did not like sweet potato, and she liked the idea of having to eat it, whether she wanted it or not, still less, and the clouds began to gather on her face. She glanced about the table, and saw that Ruby was having a hard time, trying to eat a dish which she did not like, and that some of the other girls did not look very happy when they heard the rule.

Mrs. Boardman whispered a few encouraging words to Maude, and the little girl reflected that as long as she had really tried to be good about some other things, she might as well try to be good about this rule, too, and so she managed to eat the small piece of potato without saying anything about not liking it. After the girls had eaten the portion which was put upon their plates the first time, they were at liberty to decline any more for that meal; so you may be sure that Maude did not take any more.

"Don't let me forget to tell you about a boy I heard about who had to eat something he did n't like, and came very near having to make his whole dinner upon it," whispered Mrs. Boardman. "I don't think you can imagine how it happened, and you can think about it while you are eating your potato. See, it is only a little piece, and it will soon be gone. If I were in your place, I would eat it all up first, and then you will enjoy the rest of your dinner more when you do not have it to think about."

Ruby did not so very much mind anything that she had to eat at dinner; but two mornings in the week, Tuesday and Friday, there was always egg-plant for breakfast, and for some weeks Ruby would think about it all the day before, and talk about it the day after, until Aunt Emma told her that she might as well eat eggplant for every meal every day, she thought and talked so much about it.

"But I do hate it so," Ruby would say. "I don't see the use in having to eat what one does n't like. I just can't bear it, Aunt Emma."

"But you will learn to like it after a while," Aunt Emma said. "Miss Chapman thinks that little girls ought to learn to like everything that is put before them, and she tries to have a pleasant variety, and not have anything that the girls will dislike. You will see how much easier it will be to eat your piece of egg plant in two or three weeks."

"And it just seems as if I always did get the very largest piece of all," Ruby said in despair. "This morning you had a little teenty piece and mine was twice as large."

"That was so you would have twice as much practice in learning to like it, I suppose," Aunt Emma said with a smile.

After dinner was over there was a half-hour for play and then the school-bell rang, and the girls went back into the school-room. Some of them took music lessons, and they went one at a time to take a lesson in the parlor from Miss Emma.

Ruby was to take music lessons, to her great delight. She had been sure that it would be very easy, and she was quite disappointed when she found how much she would have to learn before she could play as her aunt did.

When school was over for the afternoon, at four o'clock, Ruby breathed a long sigh of relief. The day had seemed a very long one to her, though it had been very pleasant, and it seemed as if it could not be possible that only yesterday at this time she had been on her way to school.

"What do we do next?" asked Ruby of one of her schoolmates, as they went into the house together.

"We all go out together for a walk," answered the little girl. "Will you walk with me to-day? I will come to your room as soon as I am ready."

"All right," Ruby answered, and she ran upstairs to her own room, to put on her hat and jacket.

Every pleasant day the girls were taken out for a walk, and the teachers took turns in going with them. To-day Mrs. Boardman was going to take them, and Maude was very glad, because she had obtained permission to walk with her. All the girls were very fond of Mrs. Boardman, and they would obtain her promise to walk with them so many days ahead that she could hardly remember all the promises she had made.

When they were all ready they started out, Ruby and Agnes Van Kirk at the head of the little procession and Maude and Mrs. Boardman at the end.

Ruby felt very important as she looked up at the window and waved good-by to her aunt. It was great fun going out to walk this way, with a whole string of girls behind her, instead of going down the road with a hop and a skip and a jump to Ruthy's house. If Ruthy could only be here, and if at night she could kiss her mother and father good-night, Ruby was quite sure that she would think boarding-school quite the nicest place in the world.

They had a very pleasant walk. They went down the winding road, bordered upon either side with wide-reaching elm-trees, and then turned down towards the river. After they reached the path that wound beside the water Mrs. Boardman let the girls break their ranks, and run about and gather some of the wild flowers and feathery grasses that grew there in such profusion.

Ruby gathered a beautiful bunch of plumy golden-rod for her Aunt Emma, and when she went to look for Agnes, she displayed it triumphantly.

"Just see what a beautiful bunch of goldenrod I have," she exclaimed in delight. "Won't Aunt Emma be pleased? But have n't you got any flowers, Agnes? Why, what have you been doing? I thought you were looking for flowers too."

Agnes opened a paper bag, which she had loosely twisted together at the top, and which seemed to be empty, and said,—

"No, I did not get any flowers, but just see what a beautiful caterpillar I have. Is n't that lovely?"

Ruby peeped into the bag, and saw a large mottled caterpillar walking about upon a leaf, apparently wondering where he was, and doubtless thinking that the sun had gone under a cloud, since he could not see it anywhere.

"Is n't he a beauty?" repeated Agnes, in delighted tones, taking another look at her prisoner herself, and then twisting the bag together again.

Ruby hesitated. She did not like to say that she thought it was the very ugliest caterpillar she had ever seen, and that if Agnes really wanted a caterpillar she would have thought that one of the fat brown ones that she could find anywhere around the school would have been nicer, and yet Agnes seemed to admire it so much she really felt as if she ought to say something.

"Well," she said at last, as she found that Agnes was waiting for her, "I think it is certainly one of the biggest caterpillars I ever saw. What are you going to do with it? I don't see what you like caterpillars for."

"Oh, it is n't for myself," Agnes answered. "It is for Miss Ketchum. She is very fond of studying about bugs and caterpillars and everything of that kind, and nothing makes her quite as happy as to have a nice new caterpillar to watch."

"What does she do with them?" asked Ruby.

"She puts them in little boxes with thin muslin over the top, or mosquito netting, so that she can look through and watch them, and she feeds them every day with leaves or something else that they like, and then after a while they spin themselves all up into cocoons, and go to sleep, and then by and by a beautiful butterfly comes out. Oh, Miss Ketchum just loves caterpillars."

"I wish I had a caterpillar for her," said Ruby. "Well, I will get one for her the very next time I see one, as long as she likes them so much. I never heard of any one liking caterpillars before, though, did you?"

"No, I don't know as I did," said Agnes. "But I think I shall like them very much too before long, for I like to watch the butterflies come out, and I like to keep looking out for new caterpillars. I don't think I would like to bother taking care of them as Miss Ketchum does, but perhaps I won't mind that after a while. She has such a nice book about them."

Miss Ketchum was very much pleased with the new specimen when Agnes gave it to her, after the girls got home from their walk, and Ruby looked with great interest at the little boxes in which captive caterpillars were walking about, apparently feeling at home and very happy as they nibbled at their nice fresh leaves, or sunned themselves upon the netting.

"Isn't Miss Ketchum nice?" said Agnes, as the girls went up to their own rooms. "Some of the girls don't like her as well as they do the other teachers, but I do. She is always so kind about helping one with lessons, and she never gets cross unless she has one of her bad headaches, and then I should think she would be cross, for the girls tease her. She was so kind to me when I first came that I just love to get her caterpillars or do anything else I can for her."

"She was so glad to get that new one, was n't she?" said Ruby. "I will help you get some for her, Agnes, the very next time we go out walking. We will walk together, and then we can both watch for them."

"That will be ever so nice," said Agnes. "You see most of the girls make fun of Miss Ketchum because she wears those little curls on her forehead, and is absent-minded sometimes, and likes caterpillars so much, and it will please her ever so much if you like her, and help her instead of laughing at her."

It had not occurred to Ruby before that she could please any of the teachers by showing them little kindnesses and being thoughtful of them, and she remembered remorsefully how she had laughed during recess when one of the girls had drawn on her slate a funny caricature of Miss Ketchum, with the two little curls that she wore on each side of her forehead standing up like ears, and her glasses on crookedly. She made up her mind that she would never laugh at her teacher again, but try to help her in every way she could by being good herself and setting others a good example.

CHAPTER XVIII.

MISADVENTURES.

By the time Ruby had been at school a week she was quite happy, and had been so good that Aunt Emma wrote home to her father and mother that no one could ask for a better little girl, or one who made more progress in her studies.

In fact, Ruby had begun to be quite proud of herself for being so good, and quite enjoyed comparing herself with some of the other girls, who could not learn their lessons as quickly as she did, and who did not try so hard to be good and not give the teacher any trouble.

If Ruby's mother had been with her she would have warned the little girl that this was the very time for her to be most watchful lest she should do wrong, for it was generally when Ruby had the highest opinion of herself that her pride had a fall.

If any one had told Ruby upon this particular morning that she should laugh out loud in school, and more than that, laugh at Miss Ketchum, she would not have believed it, and yet that is just exactly what she did. Still, I think you will hardly blame Ruby when I tell you how it happened.

It was quite true that, as Agnes had said, Miss Ketchum was apt to be absent-minded sometimes. She was so interested in her studies that she sometimes forgot about other things, and while she never forgot anything connected with her scholars' lessons, yet she sometimes forgot little matters about her dress.

She wore her hair in a rather unusual way, and when it was brushed back and arranged she would pin a little round curl upon either side of her face. This morning she had somehow forgotten to pin one of these curls on, and as soon as the girls noticed it, they were very much amused.

If Miss Chapman had noticed it when she opened the school she would probably have reminded Miss Ketchum of it, but she did not see it, and none of the girls told her; so the curl was still missing when Ruby went up with the rest of the class to the desk, to recite her grammar lesson.

She was not quite sure that she knew it, and she had been studying so hard up to the last minute that she had not noticed how the other girls had been laughing behind their books and desk-covers, and had not even looked at Miss Ketchum since school began.

Ruby was at the head of the class, and so the first question came to her,—

"What is an adverb?"

Ruby looked up at her teacher, and was just about to answer, when her eyes rested upon the place where the curl ought to have been. Miss Ketchum's hair was very thin just there, and the contrast between the round curl on one side of her head and the empty place upon the other was so funny that before Ruby thought of what she was doing she had laughed aloud.

Miss Ketchum had not the least idea that there was anything in her appearance which could be amusing, and as she had often been tried by mischievous scholars giggling or whispering, she thought that Ruby was deliberately intending to be rude, and very naturally she was much provoked at her. One could hardly have expected her to think anything else, for it was not very pleasant to have one of her scholars look straight at her and then burst out laughing.

Poor Miss Ketchum's face grew as red as Ruby's own, and she said very sternly,—

"I am surprised at you, Ruby. I did not know that you could behave so badly. You may carry your grammar over there in the corner, and sit there facing the school the rest of the day. Next, what is an adverb?"

Poor Ruby was too miserable to try to explain, and she did n't like to tell Miss Ketchum that she had left her curl off; so she took her book and went over in the corner, feeling completely in disgrace.

After a while the door opened, and Aunt Emma looked in, to call one of her pupils for her music lesson, and the look of grave surprise upon her face when she saw Ruby sitting there by herself made the little girl more miserable than ever. She had not meant to laugh. If she had noticed the missing curl before she came to the class she never would have laughed; but seeing it suddenly drove the adverb quite out of her head, and before she had known what she was about she had laughed.

It seemed a long time to recess, and it was all that Ruby could do to keep the tears out of her eyes. It was the first time in her life that she had ever been in disgrace at school, and she felt it keenly. It would have been bad enough if it had happened in school at home, but to have it happen here was doubly hard.

Ruby was sure she could never be happy here again, never, after having to stay up there all the morning in disgrace before the whole school.

At last the recess-bell rang, and the other scholars went out to play, and Ruby and Miss Ketchum were left alone.

"I shall hear your grammar lesson in a few moments, Ruby," said Miss Ketchum, in a stern tone, and she went to her room, leaving Ruby with her grammar in her hand, trying to keep the tears out of her eyes long enough to study.

She did not know nor care just now what an adverb was, and it is very hard to study with a great lump in one's throat, and tears in one's eyes. If she had really meant to be mischievous it would not have been so hard to be in disgrace, but Ruby really had not intended to do wrong, and she would not have done anything to make Miss Ketchum feel badly for anything in the world if she had had time to think. Agnes had cast a pitying glance at her as she went out, for she had understood how it was, and she hoped that during recess time, when Ruby and her teacher should be alone together, Ruby would tell Miss Ketchum why she had laughed.

After Ruby's punishment none of the other girls had shown that they noticed the missing curl, lest they should be sent up to the platform too, for speaking about it, so Miss Ketchum did not discover her loss until she went to her room at recess.

The first thing she saw when she entered her room was a dark curl lying upon her bureau. She looked at it wonderingly for a moment, and then put her hand up to her head. One curl was in its place, but there was the other lying upon the bureau. She had forgotten to put it on. Looking at herself in the glass, Miss Ketchum smiled, although she was very much mortified to think that she had been in school all the morning without knowing that she had not finished dressing. She understood Ruby's behavior then.

Going back to the school-room she sat down at her desk and called Ruby to her.

"Ruby, dear, you did not intend to be disorderly this morning in class, did you?" she asked.

Ruby burst into tears, and hid her face. In a moment Miss Ketchum's arm was about her, and she was crying on her teacher's shoulder.

"Indeed I did n't," she answered, between her sobs. "I never thought of such a thing. I was just going to tell you what an adverb was, and when I looked up I saw—I saw—"

"That my hair was not arranged properly?" asked Miss Ketchum.

"Yes'm," said Ruby, "and then before I knew what I was going to do I had laughed. I am so sorry, and oh, I wish I could go home. I never was bad in school before, and I did not mean to be this time. Indeed I am so sorry I laughed, Miss Ketchum. I could n't help it and I did n't know I was going to, truly I did n't."

"Ruby, dear, I feel as if it was more my fault than yours," said Miss Ketchum, gently wiping away the little girl's tears. "Now you may go out to play and I will hear your lesson some time after school, when you feel like coming up to my room to say it, and you shall have your good mark, if you know it, just as if you had recited it in class. I shall not consider that you have done anything wrong this morning, for I can understand that you would not have laughed if you had had time to think about it for a moment. But you will try after this always to be quiet, will you not?"

"Yes 'm," answered Ruby, earnestly, and returning Miss Ketchum's kiss, she wiped her eyes and ran out to play, happier than she had had any idea that she could ever be again.

She thought to herself that she would never smile again in school, even if such a thing should happen as that Miss Ketchum should leave both of her curls off at once. When she went out to play she found that the girls were disposed to make much of her for her trouble of the morning.

"It was too bad for anything, Ruby Harper, that you had to get into trouble all on account of Miss Ketchum's curl," said one of the girls. "I don't wonder you laughed. If you had seen it before you might have been able to help it, but to look up and see her hair looking that way was enough to make any one laugh, whether they meant to or not.

"Miss Ketchum knows now that I did not mean to," Ruby answered. "I truly could not help it, but you see if I am ever in disgrace again."

"Never mind, all the girls knew how it was," answered her friend, comfortingly. "Come and play puss in the corner. I am glad she let you out instead of keeping you in all recess."

Ruby was quite happy again now, and when she had a moment in which to run up and tell Aunt Emma that Miss Ketchum said that she had not really done anything naughty, she felt much better.

But she was sorry that she had laughed, even if she did not intend to, and she wanted to make up to Miss Ketchum for her seeming rudeness; so she made up her mind that that very afternoon she would gather all the caterpillars she could find anywhere, and give them to Miss Ketchum, to show her how sorry she was, and how happy she would like to make her.

That afternoon, as soon as she had finished practising, she took an empty cardboard box, and went down to the end of the garden. She was quite sure that in the vegetable garden she would find ever so many caterpillars, and there they were,—great brown ones, crawling lazily about in the sun, smaller green ones, that travelled about more actively, and upon the tomato-plants Ruby found some that she was quite sure Miss Ketchum would like, because they were so remarkably large and ugly.

She was a very happy little girl as she filled her box, feeling almost as delighted as if she was finding something for herself with every caterpillar that she captured and put into her box.

After she had put as many as thirty or forty in their prison she found it was quite hard to put one in without another coming out, and she did not get along quite as fast. Before the bell rang for study hour, however, she had captured fifty-five, and fifty-five caterpillars looked like a great many when Ruby carefully opened one side of the box and peeped in. Ruby wrote upon the top of the box, in her very best hand, "For Miss Ketchum, with Ruby's love," and then she punched little holes in the cover that her caterpillars might have some air to breathe.

She ran upstairs to Miss Ketchum's room, which was over one end of the schoolhouse, and knocked at the door, which was partly opened. No one answered, and Ruby knocked again. She pushed the door open a little farther and looked in, and found that Miss Ketchum had gone out. She was to have charge of the study hour that afternoon, and she had probably gone downstairs. Ruby laid the box on the bureau, and ran away as the bell rang to call the scholars together, feeling quite delighted at the thought of Miss Ketchum's happiness when she should find so large an addition to her "menagerie," as the girls called it. She thought she would not tell Miss Ketchum about it, but let her have the pleasure of a surprise when she should go up to her room. Of all the little girls, no one studied more diligently than Ruby that afternoon, for she wanted to make up for the morning in every way that she could; and the thought of the caterpillars walking about in their prison, all ready to make Miss Ketchum happy when she should find them, made Ruby very glad; so she felt like singing a little song as she studied her grammar, and looked out the map questions in her geography.

The day which had begun so disastrously was going to have a very pleasant ending after all, and Ruby no longer felt as if she must go home. When the girls had come into the school-room after recess Miss Ketchum had said what Ruby had not in the least expected her to say, that she had found out why Ruby laughed, and if she had known sooner she would not have sent her out of the class for it, as she felt as if it was her own fault instead of Ruby's, and that therefore, she should give Ruby perfect marks for deportment, since she had not intended to make any disorder during school-time. Ruby was so grateful to Miss Ketchum for thus clearing her before the school that she made up her mind that she would never, never give her teacher the least bit of trouble, but would always be good, and learn her lessons perfectly, so that she should never have any occasion to reprove her.

CHAPTER XIX.

SURPRISES.

When Ruby went to bed that night her last thought was of the caterpillars and of the pleasure they would give her teacher, and she was impatient for the morning to come that she might have Miss Ketchum tell her how much she had enjoyed them.

Miss Ketchum did not go up to her room after study hour, but after supper she went up for something, intending to return to the sitting-room at once, as she had charge of the girls that evening. It was almost dark in her room, but she did not stop to light the lamp, as she knew where to get her work-basket in the dark. In passing the bureau she put out her hand and knocked something off, but stooping down on the floor and picking it up again, she concluded that it was merely an empty paper-box, such as Mrs. Boardman often put in her room when she found one, to use as a home for her pets. The cover rolled away, but Miss Ketchum did not stop to look for it, and went down to the sitting room again.

Of course you can guess what happened. Whether the caterpillars were asleep or not when the box fell, I could not tell you, but after that they were certainly very wide-awake, for they travelled out of the box and all over the room. Before Miss Ketchum had come up to go to bed they had made their way all over the room. There were some of them on the ceiling, some crawling over the white counter-pane on Miss Ketchum's bed, some upon her pillow, and a very fat, large caterpillar, that Ruby had found upon a tomato-plant, had crept up on the looking-glass and had gone to sleep there.

Miss Ketchum was very much interested in caterpillars, but of course she did not want to have them walking all about her room in this way; so you can imagine how surprised and perhaps a little frightened she was when she came upstairs to bed, and struck a light, and saw the caterpillars making themselves quite at home all about her room. She could not understand it at first, and then it occurred to her that perhaps some of the girls had been playing a trick upon her, and had put them in the room to annoy her. Some of the scholars were unkind enough to tease Miss Ketchum sometimes, and it would not have surprised her if this had been the case to-night.

At last she remembered the box, and picking up the cover, she saw written carefully upon it, "With Ruby's love," and then she knew how it had happened.

Ruby had put them there to please her, and if the cover had stayed on the box, the caterpillars would have been quite safe, and would have been in their prison yet; but she remembered having knocked the box down, and it was undoubtedly then that they strayed out and wandered about the room.

Poor Miss Ketchum! She sighed as she looked about the room. She could not go to bed and perhaps have the caterpillars creeping all over her in the night, and yet it seemed like a hopeless task to catch them, and she had no idea how many there were.

But Ruby had meant to be so kind that she thought more of her little scholar's affection for her than she did of the work she had so unintentionally given her.

One by one she patiently captured them and returned them to their box. She was not quite sure that she had got them all when she put the last one in, but there were so many that she felt tolerably certain that Ruby could not possibly have found more in one day.

It was quite late before she finally got to bed, and while Ruby was sound asleep and dreaming of Miss Ketchum's delight when she should find the addition to her pets, Miss Ketchum was smiling to herself as she thought of Ruby's intended kindness, and how it had turned out. She made up her mind that Ruby should not know that the caterpillars had escaped, but that she should think that her gift had given all the pleasure that it was intended to, and so Ruby never knew of poor Miss Ketchum's caterpillar hunt at bed-time.

The next day Miss Ketchum thanked her for them, and explained to her that she would have to set some of them at liberty again, since she had some of a good many of the varieties, and two of each were all that she could take care of; but Ruby was delighted to hear that Miss Ketchum had never had some of the specimens before, and that shc was quite sure that they would make beautiful butterflies.

After this Ruby and Miss Ketchum were as good friends as Agnes had always been with her teacher, and Miss Ketchum found it a great help to have two little girls, instead of one, upon whom she could always rely for good behavior, and who could be trusted never to wilfully annoy her.

She had a great many treasures in her room that had been brought to her from China by a brother who had been a missionary there, and she was always glad to have Agnes and Ruby come and pay her a little visit, and look at whatever they wished. She knew they could be trusted to handle things carefully and not be meddlesome, and many a happy hour the two girls spent there. Miss Ketchum's room was a very large room, as it was the only one over the school-house, so she had plenty of space to keep all her curiosities and her pets.

There was a little cupboard that stood in a corner, just as if it had been built for that particular space, and in this corner closet Miss Ketchum kept a little tin of delicious seed-cakes, and some cups and saucers, and pretty little plates with butterflies, and mandarins, and pagodas, and Chinese beauties upon them; and very often when the girls came to see her she would open this cupboard and they would have a little treat, which seemed all the more delightful because the plates were so odd. There was an open fireplace in the room, and when the days were cold and there was a snapping, blazing wood-fire, they used to ask Miss Ketchum if they might not bring their chestnuts and roast them in the hot ashes.

Miss Ketchum knew a great many stories, too, and sometimes, on Saturday afternoon, when the children had plenty of time, and would surely not have to hurry away in the most interesting part of the story, she would lean back in her big rocking-chair, and with the little girls sitting on ottomans, one each side of her, she would tell them delightful stories about when she was a little girl and went to school. Ruby and Agnes were glad that they did not live then, when there was no whole holiday on Saturday, but they were very much interested in hearing all that Miss Ketchum had to tell them, and in comparing the things that she did when she went to school with what they did themselves.

Altogether Miss Ketchum was a very delightful friend to have, if, she was a little forgetful sometimes, and did like caterpillars; but Ruby and Agnes grew almost as fond of her pets as she was herself, as they learned how much there was of interest about them. They looked forward quite eagerly to the time when, instead of the ugly worm that had woven a chrysalis about himself and gone to sleep for the winter, there should burst forth a beautiful butterfly. It made them more careful not to hurt creeping things, and if they found a brown worm crawling about where he might be stepped upon, the girls would always pick him up carefully upon a stick or leaf and put him in a safe place where he might keep out of danger.

CHAPTER XX.

PERSIMMONS.

The September days passed away and the October days came and found Ruby both happy and good. She had not forgotten her home nor her dear mother and father, but she was learning to love her new home very dearly, and she had tried so hard to be good and give the teachers as little trouble as possible that they were all very fond of her. She found her lessons very pleasant, and as she loved study and was ambitious to always have perfect lessons she was very near the head in all her classes.

Twice a week she wrote long letters home to her mother, and told her all about her doings; and her mother was so much better that she was able to write to Ruby two or three times a week,—such loving letters that Ruby always wished for a little while that she could put herself in an envelope and send herself home to her mother, instead of waiting for Christmas. Ruby was doing so well that both her Aunt Emma and her father and mother wanted her to stay until the end of the term at any rate. Ruby hoped that when she went home she would be able to take with her at least one of the five prizes which were to be given at Christmas. There was a composition prize, a deportment prize, a prize for grammar, one for spelling, and one for improvement in music. Ruby had worked so hard in all her classes, and had been so careful to keep all the rules, that she was quite sure that she should take at least one prize home with her to show her father and mother how hard she had tried to be good.

If Ruthy could only have been with her, Ruby would have been quite contented; but with all her new friends she still missed the dear little friend who had been like a sister to her all her life.

A great many things that had seemed hard to Ruby when she first came were becoming so natural to her now that she never thought anything about them. The courtesying was no longer any trouble to her; on the contrary, she really liked it, and she amused her Aunt Emma one day by telling her that she thought that when she went home she should always courtesy to her father and mother when she went out of the room; for if it was respectful to courtesy to her teachers, it was certainly respectful to courtesy to any one else of whom she thought a great deal. She had learned to like egg-plant just as well as she did anything else, so her trouble over that had melted away into thin air; and she had found Agnes Van Kirk a very good friend to have, for she was a little girl who tried very hard to do right herself, and helped Ruby to do right, too.

Agnes was going to be a teacher some day, she hoped, and she was very fond of talking to Ruby about her plans. She was going to have a large boarding-school, and she was not quite sure whether she would have her girls courtesy or not when they went out of a room.

"Perhaps it will be old-fashioned by that time, you know," she said to Ruby, when the two girls had counted how many years must pass away before Agnes should have completed her education and opened her school. "Of course I should not teach my girls to do old-fashioned things, that would make people laugh at them, but I want them to do everything that is nice. I mean to be such a teacher as Miss Chapman. She never scolds, but all the girls mind her, and even those who break the rules always wish they had n't when she looks at them. I can hardly wait, I am in such a hurry to begin my school."

"And I will come and see you, and look at the girls the way that lady looked at us the other day when she came to visit the school," said Ruby. "Do you remember how beautifully she was dressed, Agnes, and how pretty she was? I wonder if she meant to send her little girl here, and that was why she came. Won't it be fun to go and visit your school when I don't have any of the lessons to study, nor anything. I will be very grand, and they will never guess that we used to be little girls and go to school together. I don't want to be a school-teacher, though."

"What do you want to be?" asked Agnes.

"I think I shall write books," announced Ruby.

"Why, what ever made you think of that?" asked Agnes, in astonishment. "You don't even like to write compositions, and how could you ever write books?"

"Oh, compositions are different from books," returned Ruby, airily. "I am sure I could write poetry, I like it so much. There is n't anything I like better than poetry day. I wish it was poetry day every Friday, instead of every other one being compositions. I don't think compositions are at all interesting. We have to write a composition for next time upon one of our walks. I think I will write about our walk this afternoon. I don't think there is ever very much to write about the walks we take. We just go out two and two, and we see the same things every time, and that is all there is of it."

"Perhaps something may happen to-day to give you something to write about," Agnes answered; and though she had only spoken in fun, without any idea that her words would come true, something did happen that afternoon, quite out of the usual course, and I am not sure but that Ruby would have rather that it had not happened, and that she would have had less to write about.

Miss Ketchum announced at the close of the afternoon school that the girls would go for their walk half an hour earlier than usual, as they were going to gather persimmons, and would want to have more time than for their regular walk.

This gathering of persimmons was a treat looked forward to by the girls, and they were very much pleased when they heard that they were to go this afternoon. They each had a little basket in which to bring home their spoils, and Ruby was quite as excited as the rest of them, wondering whether she would find enough to fill her basket. It was the first of November, and there had been several slight frosts, which, Ruby heard the teachers say, ought to ripen the persimmons.

"That is funny," she said to herself. "I should think it would spoil persimmons to be frozen. I never heard of anything being better because it had been out in the frost. I wonder what persimmons are like, anyway."

Ruby had never seen any persimmons in her life, as they did not grow near her home, and she had a vague idea that they were like apples, only smaller, perhaps. It did not take the girls very long to get ready, and in a little while they were all on their way, so happy that it was hard work to keep in procession, and not lose step with each other.

It was a beautiful day. The sky was so blue that not the tiniest little white cloud was floating about upon it anywhere, and the air was not very cold. There was just enough frostiness to make warm wraps very pleasant, and to make the girls find a brisk gait delightful.

The leaves had all dropped from the trees, and their bare, brown limbs stood out sharp and clear against the sky, and Ruby wondered whether the persimmons would not have fallen from the tree, too. She did n't ask any questions, however, but made up her mind to wait and see for herself. It was very hard for Ruby to admit that she did not know anything; and although Agnes could have told her all about the persimmons, she preferred to wait rather than ask her.

It was quite a long walk to the field where the persimmon-tree grew which was considered the special property of the school. In the woods there were several persimmon-trees, but the boys knew where those persimmons grew, and gathered them as soon as they ripened, and very often before they were ready to eat; so it was of no use going there to look for any. This tree stood in a field that belonged to a friend of Miss Chapman's, and he always kept it just for the girls, and was willing to send out his man to shake the tree and knock the persimmons down for them, if Jack Frost had not done it already. As soon as they reached the field, and the bars were let down, the girls could break their ranks and rush for the persimmon-tree, which grew in the middle of the field. It did not look very inviting, Ruby thought, as she ran along with the others. All the leaves had dropped off except a few which dangled as if the next puff of wind would send them down upon the ground with the others; and the persimmons, which hung thickly upon the branches, did not look at all as Ruby had fancied that they would.

There were several lying upon the ground, and Ruby wondered at the girls for picking them up so eagerly. They were all shrivelled, and the least touch would break their skins. Indeed some of them in falling had broken, and were lying in bunches, all mashed together. Ruby did not want any such looking persimmons as those, and she looked carefully about for nice round ones, that were firm and hard.

"Come over here, Ruby," called Agnes. "Here are ever so many, and such nice ones. I am getting lots."

Ruby glanced over and saw that those in Agnes' basket were just the kind that she did not want.

"I see some here," she answered, and so she picked up the firm, hard fruit as quickly as she could.

Presently she wondered what they tasted like, and she put one in her mouth.

Did you ever have your mouth puckered up by a green persimmon? If you have, then you will know just how Ruby's mouth felt; and if you have not, you must imagine it, for I am sure I cannot tell you about it. It was a very green persimmon that Ruby had tasted, and she had taken such a bite of it before she could stop herself that it seemed to her as though she would never be able to open her mouth again. She was quite frightened at the way her mouth felt, and her eyes filled with tears as she went over to Agnes.

"Oh, it has done something to my mouth, and puckered it all up," she said, trying to keep from crying. "I never had such a dreadful feeling in my mouth. Do you suppose it will ever come out again? Oh, it is worse than a toothache, it truly is."

"You must have eaten one that was not quite ripe," said Agnes. "Let me see; oh, that one would pucker your mouth dreadfully, for it is n't nearly ready to eat yet. See, it is only these soft ones that are ripe, and the hard ones will all pucker one's mouth."

"And I thought that these soft ones were n't good," said Ruby, in dismay, "and I have gathered only these old puckery ones. I could not think what you picked up the squashed ones for."

How many times that afternoon Ruby wished she had known more about persimmons, or that she had asked some of the other girls something about them.

Her mouth seemed to grow more puckery every moment, and she wondered whether it would ever be any better. It did not feel as if it would, and she could not be persuaded to taste a ripe persimmon, for she had had enough of persimmons. She emptied her basket out, and did not want to touch another, though the girls assured her that the ripe ones were delicious.

She was very glad when at last the girls had gathered as many as they wanted, and they were ready to go home again.

She went upstairs to her room, and Aunt Emma did what she could to relieve the puckered little mouth; but there was but little that could be done except to wait patiently for time to take the puckers out of it.

Ruby was quite sure that it would take a year, and when she woke up the following morning and found that there was nothing to remind her of the persimmon, she was delighted as well as surprised, but it was a long time before she wanted to hear any more about persimmons.

CHAPTER XXI.

MAUDE.

If Maude's mother could have looked into the school and watched her little daughter for a day, I am sure she would have found it hard to believe that she was the same child as the selfish, self-willed little girl, who had made every one else miserable as well as herself if she could not have her own way when she was at home.

School life was very hard for Maude in a great many ways, and she had been more homesick than any of the other girls,—not so much because she wanted to see her father and mother as because she wanted to go where she could have her own way and do as she pleased.

All her life she had been accustomed to having her own way, and after such training it was very hard for her to submit to the same rules to which the other girls had to submit, and to obey her teachers. It was a new experience to her to find that her fine clothes did not win for her any esteem, and that unless she showed herself kind and obliging to her schoolmates, they did not care to have anything to do with her.

It was not altogether Maude's fault that she had been so selfish; it was partly because she had never been taught to be unselfish, and she had grown so used to putting herself and her own comfort before that of every one else, that it seemed the most natural thing in the world to do, and she was surprised when every one else did not do so too. Nothing could have been better for her than to come to this quiet home school, where she could find a friend who would take the trouble to help her correct her faults as Mrs. Boardman did.

Maude had never really loved any one before in all her life. She had valued others only for what they did for her, but now she was learning to love from a better reason than that. She really tried to please Mrs. Boardman by obeying the rules and trying to study her lessons, and though it was hard for her to keep up with her class, Mrs. Boardman encouraged her because she could see that Maude was really doing her best.

If Maude grew discouraged, and began to think that it was of no use for her to try to learn, that she would never be able to learn her lessons and get up to the head of any of her classes, Mrs. Boardman would tell her how much she had improved since she first came, and encourage her to try again.

For the first few weeks Maude found herself frequently in disgrace. It seemed almost impossible for her to understand that she must obey without arguing the point, and that she must not be quarrelsome nor selfish in her intercourse with the other scholars. If Maude had been in a large school where she would not have had any one to help her, she might not have improved so much; but in this little school, where it was more like a family than a boarding-school, she was helped to conquer herself just as wisely as she could have been by a wise mother.

When at last she really learned that no one cared for her father's money nor her mother's servants, nor her own jewelry, which she was not allowed to wear, and had to content herself with exhibiting, she began to wish that there was something about herself which should win the love of her schoolmates.

She had made such an unpleasant impression upon them at first that they were not very anxious to make friends with her, but as they saw that she was really trying to make herself pleasant, they were more willing to invite her to join in their games and share their amusements.

She did not talk so much about her possessions, and tried to care more about others and their happiness. But all this was hard work. It is not an easy matter to be selfish and wilful and then all at once become thoughtful of others, and of their comfort; and many and many a night Maude sobbed herself to sleep, quite discouraged with the efforts she had to make to do things that seemed to come as a matter of course to the other girls.

Mrs. Boardman had grown to love the lonely little girl, when she saw how much she needed a friend, and how grateful she was for the kindness which was shown her; and sometimes she would ask Miss Chapman to let Maude spend the night with her, when she found that the little girl was very homesick and discouraged.

Perhaps because she had never known before what it was to have a friend who really wanted to help her make the most of herself, Maude loved Mrs. Boardman with all her heart, and she really tried and kept on trying, so that she should not disappoint the one who took so much interest in her.

Mrs. Boardman could see how the little girl improved from one week to another, and though there was still much room for improvement, and it might take months and perhaps years to undo the effect of Maude's early training in selfishness, yet there was a great deal that was very sweet and lovable in her character, hidden away under all the dross; and Mrs. Boardman knew that if she kept on trying to improve, some day she would be a very sweet girl, and one who would win love from all around her.

Every hour Maude learned something that was of use to her, for she had much more to learn than many of her schoolmates. In the first place she had always thought that work was something that belonged only to servants, and that a lady would not know how to do anything about the house; but here Miss Chapman insisted upon each little girl's caring for her own room, and insisted that the work should be carefully and well done, and the general feeling among the girls was that it was something to be proud of when their rooms won commendation from Mrs. Boardman.

Maude no longer felt that it was a disgrace to be obliged to make her own bed, but on the contrary, she took a great deal of pride in making it so well that when Mrs. Boardman went around to look at the rooms after the girls had gone into school, she could find nothing to reprove, but on the contrary could leave a little card with "Good" upon the pillow.

Once a week there was a cooking-class which the girls attended in turn, and Maude was as proud as any of the other girls could have been upon the day when she made a plate of nice light biscuit all by herself, for supper; and she looked forward with a good deal of pleasure to the time when she should show her mother how much she could do.

Miss Chapman did not believe in education making little girls useless at home, but she tried to have them taught practical things as well as the more ornamental ones, for she wanted them to grow up useful as well as accomplished women.

So the scholars learned to sweep and dust, to make beds, and bread and cake, while they studied their other lessons; and when they went home in vacation times their mothers found them very useful little maids.

Maude had not made any special friends among the girls. In her time out of school hours she stayed with Mrs. Boardman as much as she could, and her teacher was very kind about letting the little girl come to her room whenever she wanted to, and curl up in the big rocking-chair and watch Mrs. Boardman as she sat by the window in her low sewing-chair and did the piles of mending which accumulated every week.

The boxes of cake and candy which Maude had been so anxious that her mother should send her were not permitted to any of the scholars at Miss Chapman's school. Perhaps one reason why they were so well, and the doctor seldom, if ever, paid any of them, a visit, was because they ate such good, wholesome food and were not allowed to spoil their appetites with candy.

Once a week they had candy, and then it seemed all the nicer because it was such a treat. A little old woman kept a candy store some little distance down the street, and the girls were allowed to go down there Saturday mornings and buy five cents' worth of candy. This little old woman was quite famous among the scholars for her molasses cocoanut candy, and they almost always bought that kind of candy.

As Ruby said to her Aunt Emma after she had been to school a few Saturdays,—

"It looks very nice, and is good, and then you get more of it for five cents than any other kind of candy, so it is really the best kind to buy, you see."

The old woman always expected Miss Chapman's young ladies every Saturday, and had nice little bags of candy all tied up, ready for them, so that she should not keep them waiting; and if the day was stormy, and she knew that they would not be allowed to go out, she took a covered basketful of candy-bags up to the school, that they might make their purchases there.

Saturday morning was a very pleasant one at school. There was a short study hour, which was really a half-hour, and then the girls wrote letters home, or visited each other in their rooms.

In the afternoon they put on their very best dresses, and had a nicer supper than usual, and almost every Saturday evening the minister and his wife came and took that meal with them.

He was not at all like the minister Ruby had known at home all her life, and whenever she looked at him, she wondered how it was possible for so young a man to be a minister. He never asked any of the girls whether they knew the catechism or not, and Ruby was quite disappointed at this, though I do not think any of the other girls wanted to say it. Ruby was so sure that she knew it perfectly, even the longest and hardest answers, that she was always glad of a chance to show how well she knew it. Perhaps if the others had known it as well, they might have been willing to say it, but as it was, they were quite satisfied that he never asked for it; and Maude, who did not know a word of it, and who had all she could do to learn what her teachers required of her, would have been quite discouraged, I am afraid, if the recitation of the catechism each week had been added to her other tasks.

CHAPTER XXII.

SUNDAY AT SCHOOL.

Sunday morning the scholars slept nearly an hour longer than usual, and this was looked upon as a great treat, particularly in the winter months when it was scarcely light before seven. It seemed very early rising to get up by lamp-light, and all the girls were quite ready to take the extra hour of sleep upon Sunday mornings.

After breakfast, which was always nicer than upon other days, when they had made their rooms tidy, and prepared themselves for church, all but their coats and hats, Miss Chapman called them down to the school-room to study a Bible lesson for half an hour.

By this time the church bell would begin to ring, and they would go up to their rooms and get ready to start, and then the little procession would start out just as they did when they went to walk, only, instead of one of the girls walking at the head, Miss Chapman and Miss Ketchum were there, and the girls followed them.

It was a very short walk, just across the street, so it was not necessary to start until the second bell had begun to ring. The girls would have been very glad if it had been a little longer walk, but it only took two or three minutes to walk down to the crossing at the corner, and then go across to the pretty vine-covered church.

Miss Chapman had one rule that none of the girls liked at all, and yet it was one for which they were all very glad when they had grown older, and did not have to follow it unless they wished.

It was her rule that the girls should all listen very attentively to the sermon, remember the text, and the chapter from which it was taken, and then when they came home they were required, after dinner, to spend an hour in writing down all that they could remember of the sermon. At first Ruby was sure that she never could remember anything to write down afterwards, and though she listened as hard as she could, and did her very best to remember, all that she could possibly keep in her head was the text, and one sentence, the sentence with which Mr. Morsell began his sermon; but she soon found that by listening very closely and trying to remember, she grew able to remember much more.

Some of the older girls, who had been with Miss Chapman for two and three years, and were accustomed to this practice, could write down a really good epitome of the sermon, and once in a while a scholar did so well that Miss Chapman would send her work over to the minister, and the next time he came to tea he would compliment her for it; and that not only pleased the scholar, but made all the others determine to do so well that their extracts, too, should be sent over to him sometimes.

Mr. Morsell always remembered what young hearers he had, and he never failed to put something in his sermon that even Ruby and Maude could understand and remember, if they tried hard enough; so it was a great deal easier for them than if he had preached only for grown-up people.

Each girl had a blank-book, and after Miss Chapman had looked her extracts over, she required the scholars to copy these extracts into their blank-books.

Ruby was quite pleased when she found that each Sunday she could remember more and more, and that where five lines contained all that she remembered of the first sermon, it soon took two pages to hold all that she could write.

She was glad that she had to copy it in this blank-book, for then she could take it home with her at Christmas, and show it to her father and mother and Ruthy; and everything that she did she always wanted to show them, or tell them about, for she never forgot the dear ones. Maude was learning to remember nicely, too. She was not at all a dull little girl. It was only that she had not been accustomed to use her mind when she came to the school, and it had taken her some little time to learn to keep her thoughts upon anything, and really study. She was quite pleased when she found that in this exercise of memory she was doing quite as well as any of the new scholars, and better than four or five of them could do.

After a while, when the girls grew older, and finished learning all that they could study with Miss Chapman, and some, perhaps, did not go to school any more, they were very glad that they had learned to listen so attentively; for any one of those little girls who practised listening to the sermon and remembering all they could of it, and then strengthened their memory by writing it down afterwards, found that they had a great deal to be glad of in this training. Even after they grew up, they were so in the habit of listening attentively that they never heard a sermon without being able to remember a great deal of it; so their memories were not like sieves, through which a great deal could run, but in which very little, or perhaps nothing, would remain.

But they did not realize then how good it was for them, for even grown-up people very seldom realize that, and so the girls grumbled a good deal sometimes, when they had to sit down on Sunday afternoon and write out what they could remember.

There was one thing, however, which the girls soon discovered. It did not make it any easier to grumble about it, and the sooner one set to work in good earnest, the more one was likely to remember of the sermon, and the sooner the task was accomplished; and they had the rest of the afternoon to themselves until Bible-class hour just before tea-time.

Then Miss Chapman heard them say the catechism, and talked to them and heard them recite the Bible lesson which they had studied that morning. The time between writing the sermon and the Bible class was always a pleasant time to the scholars. They sat in one another's rooms and talked, or if it was a pleasant day they went out and walked about the garden. While Miss Chapman would not allow any loud laughing nor playing on this day, yet she was glad to have it one which the girls would enjoy as much as possible, and would look back upon with pleasure.

There was always some special dainty for tea, and then, after tea, the girls all gathered around the piano in the parlor, and Miss Emma played hymns for them, and they sang until it was time to go to bed. They all enjoyed this. Even the girls who could not sing very well themselves liked to hear the others sing, and they were sorry when the old clock in the hall struck the bed-time hour.

Every Sunday seemed such a long step towards the holidays when they should go home and see their fathers and mothers again. While after the first week or two none of the girls were homesick, and all were very happy, yet there was not one of them who had not a little square of paper near the head of her bed, with as many marks upon it as there were days before vacation began, and every morning the first thing they did was to scratch one of these marks off. So Sunday seemed a long step ahead when they looked back over seven days that had passed.

Agnes and Ruby generally spent the leisure part of Sunday afternoon with Miss Ketchum. She was very fond of the little girls, and liked to have them come and see her, so they had a very pleasant time in her room.

They would save their bags of candy, instead of eating them on Saturday, and Miss Ketchum would have a nice little plain cake, of which her little visitors were very fond, and then they would take down the dishes and have a very nice time.

While they were enjoying the good things Miss Ketchum would read to them, or they would see which could tell her the most about the extracts they had written from the sermon. They had such pleasant times with her that they were always sorry when the boll rang for Bible class, and they had to say good-by and run away.

Altogether, Sunday was a very happy day at Miss Chapman's, not only to Ruby and Agnes, but to all the other scholars, and they were always ready to welcome it.

CHAPTER XXIII.

GETTING READY FOR CHRISTMAS.

All the girls had a great deal of Christmas preparation. In the evenings they were busy making their Christmas presents for their friends at home, and Ruby was delighted when her Aunt Emma taught her how to knit wristlets. She was very proud when she had finished the first pair for her mother. They had pretty red edges and the rest was knitted of chinchilla wool.

Perhaps you would laugh at Ruby if I should tell you quite how much she admired them. When she first began to knit she wished that she need not practise nor study nor do anything else, she enjoyed her new occupation so much; and she carried her wristlet around in her pocket, wrapped up in a piece of paper, so that it should not become soiled, and every little while she would take it out and look at it lovingly.

She could imagine her mother's surprise and pleasure when she should give them to her, and tell her that her little girl had knitted every stitch of them for her. There were a great many stitches in the wristlets, and before the first pair was finished Ruby had grown very tired of knitting; but she was willing to persevere when she thought of the pleasure it would be to give them to her mother as her very own Christmas gift to her.

The pair she was making for her father did not take her nearly so long to make, even although they were larger, for she had learned to knit so much more quickly; and she was quite proud of the way in which the needles flashed in her busy little fingers.

Ruby had brought her doll to school with her, and she found her great company when she went up to her room, although she was such a busy little maiden that she did not find much time in which to play with her. Sometimes she would take her over to Miss Ketchum's room and leave her for a few days, so that when she went there for a little visit she would find her doll waiting for her, but generally Ruby had so many other things in which she was interested that she did not find time to play with her child.

But she was making something for Ruthy's Christmas present in which she needed her doll's help very much. Aunt Emma was showing Ruby how to crochet the dearest little baby sacque and hood, for a gift to Ruthy, and as Ruthy's doll was just exactly the same size as Ruby's, Ruby could try the sacque upon her own doll every now and then, and be quite sure that she was getting it the right size.

It was a pretty little white sacque with a rose-colored border, and it was so very pretty that Ruby made up her mind that after Christmas, when she should not have so much to do, she would make another just like it for her own doll. The hood was made to match the sacque, and Ruby could hardly wait for Christmas to come when she thought of the happiness her gifts would give. She was impatient to hear Ruthy exclaim with admiration over the beautiful sacque and hood, and to see how proud her father and mother would be when she slipped the wristlets upon their hands, and told them that she had taken every stitch for them with her own fingers.

But besides these home preparations, there was to be a little entertainment given at Christmas by the scholars, to which some of the people of the village were always invited, besides the friends of the day-scholars, and those of the boarding-scholars who could come. This entertainment was given the evening before the girls left for their Christmas holidays, so very often their parents came a day earlier to take them home, in order to be present at this entertainment.

It was given to show the improvement of the scholars during the term, and all the girls had some part to take in it.

To some of them this was a great trial, but Ruby delighted in showing off, and she was perfectly happy when she found that she was to take part three times. It added to her pleasure to have her father write that he would surely be there, for he was coming to bring her home, as Aunt Emma was going somewhere else for her Christmas holidays. So Ruby practised and studied with all her might, as happy and as good a little girl as you could find anywhere, enjoying school-life more every day.

Ruby was to play the bass part in a duet with one of the older girls, and she had taken lessons such a little while that this seemed a very great thing to her. She was always ready to practise, so that she should be sure to know her part perfectly, and she went about the house humming the tune, until Aunt Emma declared laughingly that she fully expected to hear Ruby singing it in her sleep.

Besides this, Ruby was to recite a piece alone, and to take part in a dialogue; so you can see that she had quite a good deal to do. She would have been quite willing to do more, however, and she looked forward very eagerly to the evening of the entertainment.

The dialogue was quite a long one, and Ruby studied it every morning while she was getting dressed, pretending that her aunt and the stove were the other two characters in the piece. To be sure, neither of them said anything, for Aunt Emma was busy getting dressed, and the stove was silent, of course; but Ruby knew what they should say, for she had studied the piece so much that she knew the other parts nearly as well as her own; so she said for them what should be said when their part came, and then repeated her own speeches. There was no danger that Ruby would not be fully prepared when the great evening came.

It did not seem possible, now that she looked backward, that she had really been away from home so long. Each day had been so full of duties and pleasures, and had passed so rapidly, that they had gone almost before Ruby knew that they had commenced, and now there were only very few marks left to be scratched out upon the girls' calendars.

Ruby was very sorry for Agnes. Her mother lived so far away that it was not possible for her to go home until the long summer vacation came, so Agnes had to spend her Christmas at school.

The teachers did all they could to make the day a happy one for her, and her mother sent her a box of presents, but still that was not of course anything like a home Christmas, and it generally made Agnes feel very badly when she heard the other girls talking about the good times they expected to have at Christmas.

"It is n't only the parties and the Christmas trees and the good times," she said to Ruby one day. "It is being away from mother that is the hardest part of it all. I always put her picture on the table when I open the box and look at the presents she has sent me, and try to pretend that she is giving them to me; but it is n't of much use. I know all the time that she is hundreds of miles away, and that she wants to see me just as much as I want to see her."

It was just one week before Christmas that a very beautiful idea came into Ruby's mind, and she was so pleased that she jumped up and spun around like a top, and caught Agnes by the waist and made her spin around, too, until both the little girls tumbled down in a heap on the floor.

"Why, Ruby, are you crazy?" asked Agnes, laughingly. They had been sitting before the fire in Miss Ketchum's room, eating chestnuts and talking about the evening of the entertainment, and both of the girls had been quiet for a little while, Agnes thinking how much she would like to have her mother at the school that night, and Ruby thinking of the pleasure with which she would watch her father while she was reciting her piece, when all at once she jumped up in this state of excitement.

"What is the matter?" asked Agnes again; but Ruby would n't tell her. "It is just the most beautiful idea in all the world," she exclaimed; "but it is something about you, Agnes, and I don't want to tell you until I am quite sure how it is going to turn out. No, you need n't ask me. I shall not tell you one single word of it. I can keep a secret when I want to, and I don't mean to tell you this one. I will only tell you that if it turns out all right you will like it as much as I do, I think. Oh, I am so full of it that I must go over and tell Aunt Emma about it; but you must not ask me to tell you, for indeed I will not."

And Ruby did not, although you may imagine that Agnes was very curious to know what it could be over which Ruby was so excited, and which concerned herself.

Ruby would only answer, "Wait and see."

It had occurred to her that perhaps her mother would be willing to let her invite Agnes to come home with her for her Christmas holidays. Ruby knew that her mother was very much better now, and she was almost sure that she would not feel as if company would tire her too much. Ruby and Agnes had been such friends, and Ruby had told Agnes so much about her home and mother and Ruthy, that she was sure that next best to going to her own home and seeing her own mother, would be going to Ruby's home and spending Christmas with Ruby's mother.

Aunt Emma thought that it was a very nice plan, and Ruby wrote that very afternoon to ask her mother about it.

It seemed to the impatient little girl as if the answer would never come; and every day she watched when the mail came to see if there was a letter for her; but in three days it came, and she was delighted to find that a little letter was enclosed for Agnes, giving her a very cordial invitation to come home with Ruby to spend her Christmas holidays.

Ruby's mother was very much pleased with the idea, and glad that her little daughter had thought of inviting her lonely schoolmate home with her; and if anything could have made Ruby happier than she was already, it was her mother's approval of her plan.

You may be sure that Agnes was delighted. It seemed almost too good to be true, at first; and when she read the kind letter from Ruby's mother, and Miss Chapman gave her permission to accept the invitation, she began to look forward to the holidays quite as eagerly as any of the other girls.

Besides the pleasure with which Ruby looked forward to Christmas on her own account, she looked forward to the pleasure she expected to give others, and I need not tell you that that is the secret of the greatest happiness in all the wide world. And so the days flew on, each one bringing the joyous home-going nearer.

CHAPTER XXIV.

FINIS.

There came a morning when the very last mark was scratched off the calendars that hung in every room in the school, and the girls knew that, long as it had been in coming, the last day before the holidays had really come.

It was a delightful day, for there was so much pleasant preparation going on.

"It is just lovely to have such a higgledy-piggledy day," Ruby exclaimed with a rapturous sigh of delight. There was a rehearsal in the morning, to make sure that all the girls were ready for the evening's entertainment; and some of the girls who were not quite perfect in their pieces of music or their recitations, had to study and practise a little while; but beyond that, there was nothing but the most delightful chaos of packing trunks, laying out dresses, and talking over plans for the next day. Every little while some one would ring the bell, and the girls would rush to see which happy girl was greeting her father or mother.

Ruby's father came about noon, and she was very much surprised, for she had not expected him until afternoon, on the same train in which she had come.

When she heard there was a gentleman downstairs to see Miss Ruby Harper, she rushed downstairs so fast that she nearly tumbled down, and ran into the parlor, quite sure that she would find her father's arms waiting to clasp her.

For a moment she did not see any one else, and she fairly cried, very much to her surprise, she was so glad to see her dear father and feel herself nestled in his arms. Then some one said,—

"Don't you see me, Ruby?" and Ruby looked around to find Ruthy, all smiles, watching to see her surprise.

"Why, Ruthy Warren!"—and Ruby fairly screamed with delight. "I never, never thought of your coming. Why, it is too splendid for anything! How did you ever come to think of it, and why did n't you tell me, and are n't you glad you came?"

"I never thought of it at all," Ruthy answered. "It was all your papa's thought, and I never knew I was coming till last night when he came over to ask mamma if I could come with him. I could hardly sleep, I was so glad, for it seemed so long to wait to see you, and it was such fun to come to travel home with you."

Perhaps there was a happier little girl in the school than Ruby that day, but I do not know how it could have been possible.

She was going home the next day to see her dear mother. She had her papa and her little friend Ruthy with her, to sympathize in her joy and be proud of her success that evening, and when she should go away in the morning she would not have to leave her new friend Agnes alone at school, but she would belong to the happy party that were going to have a delightful Christmas at Ruby's home.

Altogether I do not know what could have been added to her pleasure. The day passed very quickly, and Ruby took her papa and Ruthy for a long walk in the afternoon to show them everything pretty in the village. Her tongue went like a mill-wheel, for she had so much to tell them that she could not get the words out fast enough.

At last it was supper-time, and then began the important operation of dressing for the evening. The girls might wear their hair any way they liked this last evening, and Maude was delighted when she looked in the glass and saw her hair floating about her shoulders once more. Maude's mother was not coming till the next day, so she was not quite as happy as Ruby was.

The girls were all very much excited by the time the company began to arrive. The long school-room had seats placed in one end of it for the audience, and at the other end were seats for the scholars, for the teachers, and the piano upon which the girls were to play.

Ruby was fairly radiant with delight when the moment to begin came, and she was not troubled by any of the doubts that the other girls had that they might fail. She was quite sure that she knew her pieces so perfectly that she could not possibly forget anything; and company never frightened her, it only stimulated her to do her best.

She was so glad her papa was there, for it was so delightful to look into his pleased, proud face when she recited her piece. She could not look at him during the dialogue, but she was quite sure that his eyes were following her, and the moment she had finished she looked at him and saw how pleased his face was, and how proud he looked.

Then came the duet. Agnes and Ruby were to play this together, and they had practised it so much that they were both sure that they could play it without the music. If any one had told Ruby that in this very piece she would make the only mistake of the evening, she would not have believed it possible, and yet that was the thing that really happened.

The first bar Agnes had to play alone, then she struck a chord with Ruby and then had a little run of several notes by herself. Ruby felt very grand when the duet was announced and she walked to the piano with Agnes and seated herself. She was sorry that she was on the side away from the audience, because then her father could not see her quite as well, but then he was so tall that perhaps he could see past Agnes and watch her.

They were both ready, and Aunt Emma stood by the piano with the little black baton with which she beat time.

Ruby counted softly under her breath so she should be sure not to make a mistake. Agnes played her first notes, then Ruby came in promptly with her chord, and then, oh, Ruby wished that the floor might open and let her go through into the cellar,—she forgot that she had to wait a bar for Agnes to play her little run, and began on her bass.

It was Agnes's quick wit that saved Ruby from mortification that she would have found it hard ever to forget.

"Keep right on, Ruby. Don't stop for anything," she whispered softly.

Ruby's first impulse had been to take her hands off the keys, and perhaps run away as she liked to do when things went wrong; but Agnes' whisper reassured her, and she kept steadily on. Agnes left the run out, and started in with the air, and so no one but Miss Emma, Agues, and Ruby knew that any one had made a mistake. Of course it would have been prettier if the little run that Agnes had practised so faithfully for weeks might have been played where it belonged, but it did not really spoil the piece, and Ruby breathed a sigh of relief when the leaf was turned over, and she found that everything was going smoothly.

"You were so good, Agnes," she whispered, when they went back to their seats. "I thought that I might just as well stop as not, when I had made such a perfectly dreadful mistake. I wonder if every one knew it."

"No, I am sure no one suspected it," Agnes returned comfortingly. "No one but your aunt knew, and she could see how it happened, and I am sure she liked it a great deal better than having us stop and start all over again."

All the rest of the evening's exercises passed off very smoothly; the girls presented Miss Chapman with a handsome inkstand, and she expressed her approval of their faithfulness in study during the fall months, and then presented the prizes, and then came the part of the entertainment that most of the girls liked the best of all,—the refreshments.

Ruby was not at all sleepy when bed-time came, and she wished that she could start for home at once without waiting for morning to come, but sure as she was that she should not go to sleep all night, but that she should lie awake and talk to Ruthy, she had hardly put her head on her pillow before her eyes closed and she was sound asleep.

The next thing she knew was that her aunt was trying to waken her, and telling her that they must hurry to be ready for the train, as they had several things to do before they could start.

It did not take long to waken Ruby then, you may be sure.

And so she went home again, to find her dear mother looking almost as well as ever, and so glad to see her dear little daughter again; and she was just as happy as Ruby herself when she saw the pretty book that Ruby had won as the prize for deportment. That assured her that Ruby had indeed faithfully kept her promise of trying to be good, and that she had succeeded.

Such a happy home-coming as it was; and Agnes had so warm a welcome that she felt almost as if she belonged to the family.

But we must say good-by to Ruby here, and leave her enjoying the happy holidays which she had earned by faithful study, by trying to please her teachers in every way, and by trying to make the very best of herself and make others happy; and I am sure when you say good-by to Ruby this time, you will agree with me that she is a far more lovable little girl than she was when she tried first of all to please Ruby herself.

THE END.